CHAPTER ONE

Theakston heard it first. The ageing Bull Terrier's ears pricked up and he followed the sound with his eyes as it whizzed past. Fred, the repulsive Pug was clearly oblivious to the noise, as was Detective Sergeant Jason Smith. Smith was fulfilling a promise he'd made months earlier – to give the dogs more exercise. Something always seemed to get in the way but finally he'd managed to find the time to take them for a walk in the park down the road from his house.

Smith's life had changed drastically earlier in the year when his wife moved out. She took their four-year-old daughter with her to her parents' house. That was two months ago and she was still there. Smith had made a mistake, and now he was paying for it. His wife, Detective Constable Erica Whitton had made it absolutely clear that if she was to come home, it would be when she was ready, and it would be strictly on her terms. Smith had accepted this – he deeply regretted his temporary lapse of reason, and he was willing to wait for as long as it took.

He looked at the expression on the face of his old Bull Terrier, and could sense immediately that something wasn't right. Theakston had heard something that had disturbed him. Fred, the hideous Pug still couldn't figure out what Theakston had heard, but to be fair to the gruesome dog, his hearing was nowhere near as sharp as the Bull Terrier's.

The park was busy. It was late June and the weather was warm. Mothers were venturing out with babies and toddlers – pensioners were strolling in the pleasant sunshine and students were enjoying the fresh air. Everybody was smiling. There was a sense of promise in the air – a promise of warmer weather for a few months after the recent cold spell, a promise of positivity that only the sunshine can bring.

Smith heard a scream. It wasn't a high-pitched scream, but a much lower wail that sounded like it came from the lungs of a man. There was another scream and soon the visitors to the park rushed around in panic. *Something bad has happened* was Smith's initial thought.
He tugged at the leads and pulled the already out-of-breath dogs behind him.
"Come on," he urged.
He dragged the dogs towards where the screams were coming from. More people were rushing back and forth, their smiles now gone.
"What happened?" he asked a young woman in a tracksuit.
"I just heard the screams," she told him. "Over by the lake."

The lake was more like a large pond, but locals like to refer to it as *the lake*. Smith knew the way. He spotted a crowd of people up ahead. They were gathered around something at the edge of the lake. Smith pushed his way through and stopped when he realised what they were all looking at. A middle-aged man was lying on his back. His feet were facing upwards by the water and he was staring up at the sky. In the middle of his forehead was a black hole the size of a two-pound coin.

CHAPTER TWO

Grant Webber was the first to arrive at the scene. For as long as Smith could remember the Head of Forensics had always been the first to get there. Smith had called it in and tried his best to get the crowd of people to move away from the dead man on the edge of the lake.

"Smith," Webber said. "Why is it you keep finding yourself in places where people end up dead?"

"Good morning to you too, Webber," Smith said. "I did what I could to keep these people away from the scene, but I've got these two to try and control, and it wasn't easy."

He nodded to the two dogs at his feet, both of which were now snoring loudly.

"Why can't you have normal dogs like everybody else?" Webber said. "They have to be ugliest creatures I've ever seen."

"Don't say that too loud – They might be asleep but they can still hear you."

"Well, I hope you didn't let them anywhere near the body," Webber said. "All I need right now is to waste time discarding dog hairs."

Two PC's approached them with DS Bridge and DC Yang Chu close behind.

"About bloody time," Webber said and walked up to them. "Get rid of all these people. God knows how much damage they've already done."

"Tell them they're not to go too far though," Smith added. "We'll need to speak to all of them."

The two PC's set about clearing the crowd of people, and soon afterwards Webber was allowed to work in peace.

"He's in a good mood this morning," Bridge said to Smith.

"I prefer him like this," Smith said. "It unnerves me when Webber is civil. It's not quite right somehow."

"What have we got?" Yang Chu asked.

"Dead male," Smith told him. "I was here walking the dogs when people started screaming."

"What happened to him?"

"I have no idea. The screaming started so I went to take a look and found him lying by the water. He has a huge hole in his forehead."

"Bloody hell," Yang Chu said. "Was he shot?"

"Looks like it."

"Then we're going to need to speak to everyone in this park," Bridge said. "It's busy, but someone must have seen something if he was shot."

Smith looked around him. He'd been coming to this park for as long as he could remember – it was one of his daughter's favourite places, and now a man had been killed here in broad daylight surrounded by hordes of people.

"Hold these, will you?" He handed Yang Chu both dog leads and walked over to Grant Webber without giving Yang Chu a chance to argue. Webber was crouched over the dead man next to the lake.

"What do you think?" Smith asked.

"That's quite a hole he has in his forehead," Webber replied without looking up. "And there's not much blood on his face, but if I were to hazard a guess, I reckon there won't be much left of the back of his head."

"What are you saying?"

"This looks like the work of a high calibre weapon," Webber stood up and looked around.

He walked towards a cluster of trees. The branches were hanging over the bank of the lake. A lone mallard darted out from the edge and hurried towards the middle of the lake.

"There it is," he pointed to something on the trunk of one of the trees.

"What is it?" Smith asked.

"We'll have to check, but I'd say that's a mixture of the back of the poor man's head and half the brains that were inside it."

"Good God," Smith took a closer look.

The bark of the tree was glistening in the sunshine. A clear indentation had been made around a metre from the ground and now hair, blood and brain matter were drying in the warmth of the day.

"What kind of gun would cause this much damage?" Smith asked.

"We'll find out. The bullet has to be lodged inside the tree trunk somewhere. One of my technicians is on the way, so I'll give her the job of sifting through this gore to see if she can find it."

"You're all heart. Do we know who he is?"

"All in good time," Webber said. "I'm not done here yet, and I'd prefer it if you left me in peace to do my job."

"Of course," Smith said. "One more thing though."

Webber sighed.

"What are you up to this evening?"

"What?"

"What I just said. What are your plans for this evening?"

"I haven't made any," Webber said. "I very rarely have plans these days."

"Me neither," Smith said. "How about a couple of pints in the Hog's Head? And a bite to eat."

"What for?"

"To let me help you work on your social skills. Look, Webber, we're both technically on our own right now. I'm getting pretty fed up of spending my evenings in front of the TV listening to the sound of snoring dogs. And it'll do you good to get out once in a while. What do you say?"

"I'll give it some thought," Webber said and crouched over the dead man again.

Smith walked back to Yang Chu and Bridge. Yang Chu still held onto the two dog leads. Bridge had his arm around a young dark-haired woman. Smith frowned at him.

"This is Tanya Meek," Bridge told him. "She was standing close to the man when it happened."

Smith looked at her. Her face was a disturbing grey colour and her eyes were puffy and red. She looked like she'd been crying.

"DS Smith," he said. "Are you alright? There's an ambulance on the way – you should really get checked out."

"It was horrible," she spoke very quietly. "One minute he was standing next to the tree and next thing there was this weird noise and he just collapsed to the ground."

"Weird noise?"

"A whooshing sound," Tanya whispered. "Like the sound a dud firework makes when it's lit and goes out straight away."

"Then what happened?"

"There was a horrible crunch and he just fell to the ground. I saw the hole in his head and just stared at it. A man appeared and started to scream and then I screamed too."

"Do you know who this man is?" Smith asked.

"I've never seen him before."

"We're going to need to speak to you again, but in the meantime, I suggest you let the paramedics look you over. You're probably in shock."

Smith woke the dogs, took their leads and looked around the park. More uniformed officers had arrived, and he spotted four paramedics walking down the path towards the lake. People were still milling around, obviously unsure of what had just happened. It was one of the most chaotic murder scenes Smith had ever come across.

7

"I'm going to take these two home," he told Bridge and Yang Chu. "I'll get to the station as soon as I can. It looks like yet another day off has been cancelled."

CHAPTER THREE

Whitton arrived at the same time as Smith. Since she'd moved out, they'd agreed to keep their personal lives away from work. They were both part of the same investigative team and it would be unprofessional to allow their personal differences to enter into the equation.

"Morning," Smith caught up with her at the front entrance. "How are you?"

"I've got a cold," Whitton told him. "Laura's going through a *catch every bug that's going around* stage and I'm picking them up from her."

"You know I'm always happy to have her," Smith said.

"She's better off where she is. My parents are always glad to have her there."

"I miss her," Smith said. "I miss both of you, and it would be nice to see my daughter more than once a week."

"And what would you have done with her today?" Whitton raised her voice. "Aren't you supposed to have a day off today? You never know when you're going to be called into work. Laura is better off at Mum and Dad's."

"Point taken," Smith didn't feel like a fight.

He and Whitton had been making steady progress recently, and he was willing to hold his tongue if it meant there was a chance he could get some semblance of his old life back.

"Can I buy you a coffee?" he said.

"I'm going to check my emails," Whitton replied. "I'll see you at the briefing."

Smith needed coffee. He chose his usual one from the machine in the canteen, sat at one of the tables and took out his mobile phone. A recent photograph of Laura stared at him from the screen. Smith realised how much she was starting to resemble the person she was named after. Smith's sister had been dead for years now but seeing his daughter everyday had somehow managed to keep her memory alive. Smith knew he had to do everything he possibly could to bring his wife and daughter back home.

"Morning," Chalmers sat down opposite him. "What are you looking at?"
"Morning, boss," Smith handed him the phone. "Laura's getting so big now."
"Thank God she gets her looks from her mother. I thought you were off today."
"I was," Smith told him about the dead man by the lake.
"I heard. Do we know what happened to him yet?"
"Looks like he was shot, but from the size of the hole in his forehead, it wasn't just an ordinary gun. Webber is still down there, and we've got a whole load of witnesses to interview. What brings you in here? Escaping the Super again?"
"Old Smyth has actually been quite bearable recently," the DCI told him. "He seems a lot more chilled out these days."
"God help us all."
"I actually wanted to give you a heads-up," Chalmers' tone turned serious. "As you're well aware, you've been passed over for the DI position. Again."
"It wasn't my fault," Smith protested.
"Maybe not," Chalmers said. "But smacking your Superintendent and knocking out a detective sergeant in the space of a couple of hours didn't do you any favours in securing a promotion. You were lucky you weren't fired."
"*Lucky* is my middle name," Smith said. "A new DI has been appointed – is that what you're trying to tell me?"
"Oliver Smyth. Ex-army."
"Smyth?" Smith couldn't believe what he was hearing. "You're not telling me…"
"He's the Super's nephew, but he seems alright."
"This day just gets better and better."

"The bloke's alright," Chalmers insisted. "He's the Super's brother's kid, and like I said he's ex-army. He seems to be very smart."

"The words, smart and Smyth do not belong in the same sentence. When do we get the pleasure of meeting him?"

"Monday," Chalmers said. "I'm giving you a heads-up because he'll no doubt want to head up this new murder investigation."

"That's fine by me."

"Why don't I believe you?"

"I couldn't give a rat's arse who heads up the investigation, boss," Smith said. "As long as it's done right."

"Your way, you mean?"

Smith smiled and stood up. "Thanks for the chat, boss but I've got quite a bit of work to get through. I'll look forward to meeting this nephew of Superintendent Smyth's on Monday."

CHAPTER FOUR

Helmand Province, Southern Afghanistan
A few years earlier

"Close the bloody door," Staff Sergeant Dean Moore ordered.
Corporal George Peters was up in seconds. He put down the magazine he was reading and slammed the door closed.
It didn't help.
The sandstorm that was raging outside still found a way inside the barrack building and soon everything within a ten-metre radius of the door was covered in a thin layer of sand.
"There is one saving grace," Private Tim Darwin joined in. "There's no danger of sniper fire in that storm. They might as well be shooting blind."
"That won't stop them," Private Rob King didn't share Darwin's eternal optimism. "Those bastards are used to this kind of shit. They can probably see straight through it."
"It's forecast to clear tomorrow anyway," Moore told them. "Just in time for us to go into Musa Qala. General McNeill is adamant we take the town back, and I'm inclined to agree with him."
"Why do we even bother?" King asked. "What exactly has this got to do with us anyway?"
"That's enough," Moore said. "We'll have none of that talk. We all knew the score when we arrived, so let's just get on with it."
"Hear, hear," Darwin said.
"Sycophant," King mumbled.

The door burst open with a blast of sand and Lance-Corporal Julie Ayres came in. She was holding a bundle of mail in her arms. She slammed the door behind her and dropped the mail. The letters scattered all over the sand-covered floor.

"Shit," she said.

Private Darwin got to his feet, helped her pick up the correspondence and dusted each letter down.

"It's blowing ninety miles an hour out there," Ayres said in her broad Glaswegian accent.

"Anything there for me?" Rob King asked.

"Might be," Ayres replied. "You'd find out a wee bit quicker if you helped us pick them up."

King sighed but got of his bunk anyway and went over to help.

The letters were handed out and the ripping of envelopes was soon heard followed by silence. Private King *had* received something. It was a letter from his wife, Wendy back home in York. King had to read the letter three times before he fully comprehended its contents. He put the paper back in the envelope, folded it up and stuffed it in the pocket of a jacket hanging next to his bunk.

"I'm going to be a Dad," Private Darwin shouted. "My Olivia is pregnant."

"You poor bastard," Corporal Peters said.

He put down the letter he was reading and held out his hand to Darwin.

"Congratulations, mate. You'll make a great dad."

"Well done, Private," Lance-Corporal Ayres added.

Everyone joined in Darwin's celebration. Pats on the back were followed by words of advice and even a few hugs were offered. Staff Sergeant Moore produced a bottle of whisky and handed it to Private Darwin.

"Hand it round," Moore said. "But take it easy – we've got to be on our toes tomorrow."

Darwin took a long swig and passed it on to Corporal Peters. The smile on his face looked like it had been glued there.

"What are you hoping for?" Ayres asked. "A boy or a girl?"

"I don't mind," Darwin replied. "As long as it's got its mother's looks and my brains, I'll be happy."

"If it's a boy, you can call him Charles," Peters suggested.

Darwin didn't seem to get it.

"Charles Darwin?" Peters elaborated.

"Oh," Darwin said. "Very funny. You should be on television."

The smile was still pinned on his face.

Then Private Rob King spoke, and it disappeared in an instant.

"Are you sure it's yours?"

Everybody looked at him.

"What is your fucking problem?" Lance-Corporal Ayres said.

"I'm not the one with the problem. Look at you all – sitting here like you're all happy with your lives. We're in the middle of a war in case you've forgotten. Am I the only one who's taking this seriously?"

"You're such an arsehole, Private," Staff Sergeant Moore said. "The man's just received good news. Why can't you just be happy for him?"

"Dickhead," Corporal Peters added. "You think just because you can shoot a hole in a ten-pence-piece from half a mile away, you're better than the rest of us. Any kid with a PlayStation, could do that with an L96."

"I'd like to see you try it," King scoffed.

"Any time you want."

The door opened and Lieutenant Paul Jacobs came in. Everybody in the room stood to attention.

"At ease," Jacobs said.

He spotted the bottle of whisky Darwin was holding.

"Special occasion?"

"Private Darwin has just found out he's going to be a father, sir," Moore told him.

"Congratulations, Darwin," Jacobs said. "But I'm afraid the celebrations are officially over for this evening. The sandstorm has abated, and General McNeill has issued orders that we head for Musa Qala tonight. The Taliban has intelligence that we're preparing to strike at first light, and Mc Neill thinks we can take them off guard."

Private Darwin nodded, screwed the lid back on the whisky and handed it back to Staff Sergeant Moore.

CHAPTER FIVE

"This is what we know so far," Smith began the briefing. "A man was killed earlier today by the lake in Hove Park. We still don't know who he is – he wasn't carrying any identification, but I'm positive we'll have an ID before the end of the day. Webber is still busy at the scene, but the initial findings point to a shooting. Webber suspects a very high-calibre weapon was used and as he's somewhat of an expert where firearms are concerned, I see no reason to doubt his suspicions. As we have no idea who this man is yet or what kind of weapon was used, we'll begin by interviewing witnesses. Unfortunately, the park was extremely busy when it happened so that's going to take up quite a bit of time. Does anybody have anything to add?"
"How did someone manage to shoot a man in a park full of people?" Bridge asked.
"Webber seems to believe some kind of rifle was used," Smith told him. "This doesn't look like a close range killing, so the killer could have been hidden from sight and just waited for the right moment."
"I believe the back of the blokes head was blown clean off," Yang Chu said. "That must have been some rifle."
"We won't speculate as to what kind of gun was used until Webber and his team have finished," Smith said. "Right now, our main priority is to talk to everyone who was in the park this morning. Someone might have seen something suspicious."

"Sarge," Yang Chu said. "I believe there's a new DI arriving on Monday."
Smith nodded. He glanced over at Whitton who shook her head in response.
"That's right," Smith couldn't see any reason to deny it.
"Do we know who it is?" Bridge asked.
"We certainly do. He's an ex-army man called Oliver Smyth."
"Smyth?" Bridge, Yang Chu and Whitton said in unison.

"Chalmers gave me a heads-up earlier. The bloke's the Super's nephew, but the DCI assured me he's nothing like his uncle. Now, can we get on – DI Smyth will no doubt want to take over when he arrives on Monday but right now, I'm leading this investigation. Yang Chu, do you have that list of people who were in the park this morning?"

"Of course," Yang Chu replied.

"Let's get onto it then."

Smith stood up to indicate the briefing was over.

"How are things going with you and Whitton?" Yang Chu asked Smith as they headed for the address of the first name on the list. "If you don't mind me saying, you two seem to be getting on better these days."

"We're getting there," was all Smith felt like divulging.

He and Whitton still had a long way to go, and Smith knew it was going to take a very long time to regain her trust. He wasn't even certain she would ever be able to trust him again, but he was going to do everything he could to get Whitton and Laura back into his life.

"This is the place here," Smith looked at the print-out. "Darren Hill. Forty years old. What was a forty-year-old doing in a park on a Friday morning?"

"Maybe he works nights," Yang Chu suggested.

Darren Hill opened the door with a suspicious expression on his face. He looked Smith and Yang Chu up and down. His eyes were red and heavy black rings hung beneath them.

"Who are you?"

"Police," Smith showed him his ID. "Detectives Smith and Yang Chu. Can we have a word?"

"Is this about the dead bloke in the park?"

"Can we come inside please, Mr Hill?"

"Suit yourself. You'll have to excuse the mess. I work nights and I haven't had a chance to clear up."

Yang Chu looked at Smith with a smug grin on his face.

They made their way through to a small living room. Old newspapers were stacked against one of the walls. More, recent newspapers were laid on the two-seater sofa. Darren picked them up and beckoned for Smith and Yang Chu to sit down.

"What's with all the newspapers?" Yang Chu asked.

"It's kind of a hobby of mine," Darren said and sat down on the single armchair.

"Collecting newspapers?"

"I'm a bit of an amateur war historian," Darren said proudly. "And I'm rather pedantic with it. I collect newspaper articles centred on war – I archive them and look for patterns."

"Patterns?" Yang Chu was clearly interested.

"That's right. Patterns and anomalies. For instance, I happened to see a huge anomaly in one of the, let's say *bigger* dailies the other day. It was difficult to miss, and it totally contradicted what was printed about the hostilities in Syria not so long ago. I was even tempted…"

"Mr Hill," Smith interrupted him. "We actually have a lot to get through – a lot of witnesses to interview, so can we please carry on? You were in Hove Park this morning. Is that correct?"

"I try and run there every morning after work," Darren said.

"You said you work nights?"

"That's right. I'm a line leader at a warehouse in the industrial estate just outside the city. It's not especially taxing but it pays the bills. I finish at six and I'm usually still wide awake, so go for a run before I catch a few hours' sleep. I don't seem to need much sleep."

Those bags under your eyes tell me a different story, Smith thought.

"Do you go for your run immediately after work?" he asked.

"I come home and change first then I go. I usually get back home at around nine. What has my morning run got to do with the man who was killed?"
"Probably nothing," Smith said. "Where do you run? Do you have a set route?"
Darren Hill wasn't making any sense. Hove Hill Park wasn't very big. Smith remembered he used to run the whole park in less than an hour.
"I run the same route every morning," Darren said. "I'm a bit of a creature of habit."
"And what is that route?"
"I begin at the entrance by Gill Street then follow the path down to the lake, and then I run back up again and take the path that circles the whole park. It's a two-hour run give or take."
If you're a one-legged walrus, Smith thought.
He knew the distance was only a few miles, tops.
  "Did you notice anything odd during your run this morning?" Yang Chu asked.
"What do you mean?" Darren said.
"Anything suspicious?" Smith elaborated. "Was there anybody lurking around who seemed out of place?"
"Not that I remember. Do you know what happened to the poor man yet?"
"We're still working on it. So, you didn't notice anything odd?"
"No. I'm afraid I tend to switch off during my runs. I'm sorry I can't be of any more help."
Smith stood up. "Thank you for your time, Mr Hill. We may need to speak to you again."
"What for?"
"I'm afraid I don't know the answer to that question at this moment. We'll see ourselves out."

CHAPTER SIX

"He's lying," Smith said as they drove to the next address on the list.

"Lying about what?" Yang Chu asked.

"A few things. Did he look to you like a man who runs for two hours every morning?"

"Come to think of it, no. He looked a bit overweight to me."

"I used to run that park flat when I was younger," Smith added. "And even at a steady pace you could manage the route he described in well under an hour."

"Oh, to be young again, Sarge," Yang Chu mused.

"Cheeky bastard. I'm only thirty-six. That's not old."

"Shall we bring him in? Formally question him?"

"We don't have anything on him yet," Smith reminded him. "But we'll keep him in mind. There was something not quite right about Darren Hill."

The rest of the afternoon was spent speaking to people who had been in Hove Park that morning. When the last name was ticked off the list, Smith was exhausted. Everybody seemed to have the same story – nobody had noticed anything suspicious and Smith was no closer to understanding what had happened than he had been when they'd set off earlier.

"What a waste of time," Yang Chu stated the obvious. "I can't believe it. A man was killed in broad daylight in a park full of people and nobody noticed anything. What's wrong with people today?"

"I was there too, remember," Smith said. "And I didn't notice anything either."

"Well it still doesn't make sense. What's wrong with people these days? They don't seem to see what's happening in front of their own faces."

"Very philosophical. Let's hope the rest of the team have come up with something useful."

It was past five when Smith and Yang Chu walked through the doors into the station. Baldwin was speaking to someone on the telephone at the front desk. Smith nodded to her and walked past. Since their *indiscretion*, he'd decided it would be best to stay as far away from her as possible. He headed for his office, sat down in front of his computer and switched it on. When it finally warmed up Smith opened up his email and saw there was one from Grant Webber.

"That was quick."

Smith opened it up and read. The Head of Forensics informed him that his technician had managed to retrieve the bullet from the tree trunk and now they knew exactly what type of gun fired it. There was an attachment, so Smith clicked on it and a detailed spec sheet for an army-issue sniper rifle appeared on the screen.

"Bloody hell," Smith's heart began to pound in his chest as he read.

The rifle the cartridge was fired from was an Arctic Warfare L96. It was an army-issue sniper rifle with an effective firing range of over eight-hundred metres. The cartridge in question was a 51mm Winchester 300 which was capable of inflicting serious damage even at a range of half a mile.

Smith read further and discovered the L96 had been used by the armed forces since 1982. It had been the rifle of choice in the conflicts in Iraq and Afghanistan due to its effectiveness in adverse weather conditions. A range of accessories were available. Muzzle brakes, flash hiders and suppressors made this rifle a force to be reckoned with.

"But why the hell would someone use this rifle to kill someone in a park in York?" Smith thought out loud.

It didn't make sense.

He was reminded of a series of murders a few years earlier where football players were being picked off with a Russian sniper rifle, and he shivered. That episode had almost cost him his sanity and then his life.

Smith took out his mobile phone and brought up Webber's number. He wanted to know more about this rifle. He pressed call and instantly heard a shrill noise behind him. The Head of Forensics was standing in the doorway holding his phone. Smith ended the call.

"I've just this minute read your email. What the hell is going on?"

"It's a strange one isn't it?" Webber moved closer to the computer screen. "You see that stock. It was modified from the traditional wooden polymer stock to a much lighter aluminium one. It's rugged yet sturdy. I'd love to fire one."

"What's with your obsession with guns?" Smith asked him. "I can't see the attraction of weapons that blow holes in people."

"It's not about blowing holes in people," Webber informed him. "It's the ballistics aspect I'm fascinated with. Did you know research is in progress that aims to produce the most flawless firearm ever made? Technology that calculates minute changes in wind speed and terrain for you. I watched a thing on You Tube…"

"Webber," Smith interrupted him. "I know you're passionate about these things but you're not helping. Where would someone get their hands on one of these guns?"

"You can buy them from the internet."

"You're kidding me?"

"No. There are copies available. Authentic ones are harder to come by. But you can get them."

"Surely you need some kind of license for a rifle like that?"

"Of course. There's actually a few of them in use at the local shooting club. All above board of course."

Smith's mind was becoming bogged down with all this new information.

"I didn't even know there was a shooting club in York."

"They've won quite a few major competitions," Webber told him. "They have some very experienced marksmen there."

"Are we any closer to finding out who the dead man is?" Smith changed the subject.

His brain was now on the verge of information overload.

"Not yet," Webber admitted. "But that's your department isn't it?"

"Fair enough. And that reminds me - we were supposed to be in the afternoon briefing ten minutes ago."

CHAPTER SEVEN

"Sorry we're late," Smith spoke for Webber and himself.
Bridge, Whitton and Yang Chu were already seated. PC Baldwin was also there. Smith and Webber sat down.
"Before we go over the witness interviews, we have a match for the cartridge found in the tree trunk behind where the man was shot. I'll let Webber explain what we're looking at here."
Webber stood up and spent the next fifteen minutes going over what he and Smith had just discussed.
"That sounds like some weapon," Bridge commented when Webber had finished.
"It's a bit extreme if you ask me," Yang Chu added. "Why use a military-issue sniper rifle to kill someone in a park in York?"
"So nobody would see him," Smith thought out loud. "Isn't it obvious? This rifle has an effective range of half a mile."
"The shooter could have killed him from halfway across the city," Bridge cottoned on.
"Exactly," Smith said. "And we'll refrain from using that word please. *Shooter* sounds more *New York* than York. Now we know the weapon that was used we're one step closer. Yang Chu and me drew a blank with the people who were in the park this morning. Did any of you come up with anything?"
From the blank expressions and tired eyes around the table Smith could tell that nobody had anything to report.

"Right," Smith needed to get a bit of momentum going. "We don't have any witnesses to the shooting, but in light of this new information, we now know why."

"So, we've just wasted a whole day speaking to people who couldn't have seen anything in the first place?" Bridge scoffed.

"But we can now concentrate our efforts on where the shot was fired from," Smith pointed out.

"How are we supposed to do that?" Bridge asked.

"Webber," Smith nodded to the Head of Forensics.

"I have contacted an expert," Webber began. "A ballistics expert. I know more than most, but this lady is one of the best. I believe it is possible to pinpoint the angle of the shot as well as the distance the cartridge travelled before it hit the poor bloke in the park."

"And how long is that going to take?" Bridge asked.

"As long as it takes. My expert will be arriving tomorrow morning, so we'll know more when she gets here."

"It's getting late," Smith said. "So I suggest we make a fresh start first thing in the morning."

Nobody seemed to have any objections. The sound of chairs scraping was heard then the room became silent when everyone, but Smith and Webber had left.

"About that bite to eat and a few pints?" Smith said.

"I'm not sure I'm really in the mood," Webber replied.

"It's not a bloody date, Webber. I'm hungry and thirsty and I don't particularly feel like sitting in a pub on my own. I need to go home and feed the dogs. I'll meet you in the Hog's Head at seven."

He left the room without giving Webber a chance to argue.

* * *

The Hog's Head was reasonably quiet when Smith walked in just after seven. He knew from experience that this was the calm before the summer storm – the schools hadn't broken up yet and the tourists hadn't descended on the city in their thousands. Smith preferred it like this. He couldn't see

Marge, the owner anywhere so he went outside to the beer garden and sat down at a table looking onto the newly constructed children's play area. He lit a cigarette and waited for someone to take his order. Grant Webber was nowhere to be seen.

A waitress appeared and smiled at Smith.

"What can I get you?" she asked.

"Pint of Theakstons and a couple of menus, please," Smith replied.

"Are you on your own this evening?"

"I'm meeting a friend," Smith said.

"That beautiful girl of yours not joining you then?"

"Do I know you?" Smith was confused.

He rarely forgot a face.

"Marge is my Gran," the waitress said. "I'm helping out for the summer. We've met a few times before. I think I may have had pink hair the last time."

Now Smith remembered. "Sorry, but the brown hair suits you better. How is Marge?"

"She's been quite ill," she said. "She's not getting any younger, but she refuses to slow down. I'll organise you that pint."

Smith didn't know that Marge had been ill, but then he recalled that the last time he'd been to the Hog's Head was that fateful night when he'd bumped into PC Baldwin by chance and his whole world had spiralled out of control.

Webber sat down opposite him. "You were miles away."

"Thinking of better days," Smith stubbed out his cigarette in the ashtray in front of him. "You made it then?"

"Under severe duress. I can't stay late – Gwen is arriving early tomorrow morning and I want to be up at the crack of dawn."

"I assume Gwen is the ballistics expert," Smith said.

"Correct. She's one of the most highly-rated experts in her field."

Marge's granddaughter returned with Smith's beer.

"Could I get the same, please?" Webber asked her.

"Coming right up."

"And a couple of menus," Smith reminded her even though he already knew what he wanted to eat.

She nodded and left them in peace.

"What's this Gwen going to be able to tell us?" Smith asked Webber.

"It's quite a complex science, but basically she can calculate the bullet's trajectory as well as the angle it was fired from."

"How?" Smith was amazed.

"She'll be able to work back from where the cartridge eventually ended up. She'll take into account how deep it was embedded in the tree trunk, the initial impact on the victim, and other variables such as the victim's height, where it struck the head etc. She'll work with what we know. We know the velocity of a 51mm Winchester cartridge so the damage upon impact will give us a better idea of how far the bullet travelled. Then Gwen will look at the angle, and we ought to have a rough idea of where the gunman was when he fired the weapon, give or take a few metres."

"Can you be that accurate?" Smith asked.

"If anyone can, Gwen can. Now can we talk about something more upbeat? And what's happened to my pint?"

Marge's granddaughter arrived with two pints and two menus.

"Sorry it took so long. The barrel needed changing. I thought you'd need a refill by now."

She looked at Smith.

"Thanks," he said. "I know what I'm having to eat. Steak and ale pie."

"I'll have the same," Webber said and took a long drink of his beer.

CHAPTER EIGHT

Helmand Province, Southern Afghanistan
A few years earlier

Staff Sergeant Moore was the last to enter the RG 33. He slammed the door closed and took a seat next to Lance Corporal Julie Ayres. The engine roared into life and the mine-resistant armed vehicle eased away from the barracks. Outside it was pitch black. The driver had reduced the headlights to tiny dots and was navigating by GPS and memory alone. The Afghan winter had already crept inside the vehicle and the small group of people huddled inside were silent. The only sound was the occasional cough.

"McNeill's going for an all-out strike," Private Tim Darwin broke the silence. "I read that he reckons Richards' tactics could never work on the savages here."

"How come you know all this stuff, Darwin?" Private Rob King asked.

"I believe it helps to know what you're up against. Not that I agree with McNeill. I get the feeling he just likes blowing things up."

"I preferred it when General Richards was in charge," Lance Corporal Ayres agreed. "McNeill doesn't seem to give a damn about how many people get killed as long as he blows up the Taliban."

"Can we please change the topic of this conversation," Moore ordered.

The silence returned once more. Nobody really knew what to expect as they drove further into the night. Further towards the district of Musa Qala. Gunshots could be heard in the distance. One or two hit the side of the vehicle and bounced off. The RG carried on regardless.

It slowed down and stopped. Tim Darwin peered out of the tiny window and could see faint lights in the valley below. The gunshots were becoming more frequent now. More RGs arrived and stopped in convoy alongside them.

"What's the plan, Sarge," Darwin asked Moore. "Are we going down?"

"I don't like those ridges in the mountains on the other side of the valley," Moore pointed. "They're ideal spots for enemy snipers."

"I'll pick them off before they even see us," Private Rob King bragged and patted his trusty L96.

"I don't want you out there alone," Moore told him.

"I'll go with him," Darwin offered. "I'm not far behind him in the shooting stakes."

"In your dreams," King scoffed.

"I can do it."

"Get on to it then," Moore said. "I want snipers out first – Lieutenant Jacobs has requested aerial back-up for zero one hundred, but I want those hills cleared before I send anyone down there."

"Roger that," Darwin said.

He and Private King started to assemble their weapons. King was ready first.

"I'll beat you one day," Darwin said to him.

"Save the competition for the range," Moore said. "You're both on the same team out here. I don't want any unnecessary heroics, and you do not fire unless you have a surefire hit."

"Sarge," both men said at the same time.

They eased themselves out of the other side of the RG and dropped to the ground. A bullet ricocheted off the armoured vehicle close to Darwin's head.

"Shit," he cried out.

"They're firing blind," King reassured him. "Those Taliban shoot at anything hoping for a lucky hit."

They went their separate ways round the vehicle, and both stopped – King at the front, and Darwin at the back. King rested the barrel of the rifle on the protruding headlight and looked through the scope. He trained it on the snow-covered mountains on the far side of the valley and then adjusted the night sight. The snow instantly changed colour. It became a hazy light-green fuzz over the dark red of the mountains.
"Anything?" Darwin half-whispered.
"Not a sausage," King replied. "Hold on."
"What is it?"
"I've got movement at three o'clock halfway up. It's climbing."
A few seconds later Darwin saw it too. Two specs were ascending the ridge. They both adjusted their scopes accordingly.
"I've got a clear view," King announced.
"Me too. I'll take right, you left."
"Makes sense."
Darwin rested his finger on the trigger and concentrated on the small figure in the scope. He couldn't make out the finer features, but it appeared to be a young man.
He looked harder and realised it wasn't a young man at all – it was a boy who appeared to be in his early teens.
"They're kids," he shouted to King.
"They're Taliban," King pointed out. "There are no kids out here, only enemy soldiers. Ready?"
"I can't shoot a child."
"Do it."

    Before Private Darwin could do anything, he heard a loud bang and watched through his scope as one of the young boys fell to the ground. There was another crack and his friend went down next to him. More shots were now being fired from the other RGs in their convoys and flashes of light could be seen from all over the mountainside.

"Jesus Christ," Darwin shouted. "The place is teeming with them."

He aimed and fired. Aimed and fired.

There were more Taliban snipers than they'd anticipated, and the RG was taking more and more enemy fire. The soldiers inside the vehicle got out and crouched down behind it.

"What the hell is going on?" Staff Sergeant Moore demanded. "There was only supposed to be a handful up in those mountains. They didn't know we were going to hit them tonight."

"Obviously they did," Lance Corporal Ayres said. "I don't like this one little bit."

Private King had a perfect shot in his scope. A man all in black was setting up a shot of his own. He was taking his time about it. His rifle was pointing almost directly at the back of the RG. King's finger twitched on the trigger. The man's head filled up his scope.

But King waited.

He waited and watched. The man in black became absolutely still. King was fascinated by how a man could remain so still.

King curled his finger around the trigger once more. There was a flash of light on the other side of the valley and King squeezed the trigger. The loud crack of his rifle was followed immediately by a whooshing sound.

King's shot had hit its target. The man in black was now lying on the ground. Then King heard the screaming.

"Man down," Lance Corporal Julie Ayres bellowed. "Private Darwin has been hit."

CHAPTER NINE

"This looks good," Grant Webber looked at the plate in front of him.
A steaming steak and ale pie was begging to be eaten.
"Every time I come in here I promise myself I'm going to order something different," Smith started to cut open the thick pastry. "But I always end up with the same thing. I've become a creature of habit."
"There's nothing wrong with that," Webber said and took a bite. "Christ, this is hot."
They remained silent as they savoured Marge's pies. Webber was the first to finish.
"I can see why you don't eat anything else here. That pie could win awards."
"It's the best thing I've ever tasted," Smith said and admitted defeat by putting down his knife and fork. "And I'm sure they've got bigger over the years."

They ordered more drinks and Smith looked at his watch. It was almost nine.
"Tell me more about this gun expert of yours."
"She's not so much a gun expert," Webber corrected him. "She's more of an authority on ballistics. It's the science of projectiles. I find it intriguing to be honest."
"How exactly does it all work?"
"You'll find out more tomorrow, but what science can do now is analyse in detail the flight behaviour and impact effects of these projectiles. Twenty years ago, ballistics experts actually used lengths of string and tape measures to work out distances and angles but now we have complex computer analyses to do that in much more detail. For example, the details of the events of this morning in the park can be fed into this computer

program and we'll have a much better idea of where the bullet was fired from."

Webber was becoming quite animated. Smith wasn't sure if it was the alcohol or because he was discussing a topic he was clearly fascinated with.

"How are you doing?" Smith asked him.

"What?"

"How are you doing otherwise? It's only been a few months since the DI was killed."

Webber and Detective Inspector Bryony Brownhill had been living together for quite some time. There was even talk of marriage, and then Brownhill's life had been cut short while on duty.

"Some days are better than others," Webber said. "I miss her some days more than others, but I think I'm coming to terms with what happened. Besides, I was on my own for so long before I met Bryony, I'm used to my own company."

Smith looked at the empty glasses on the table. He picked them up and went to the bar to get two more. Webber didn't even argue.

"What about you?" Webber asked when Smith got back. "How are you finding it without Whitton and Laura at home?"

"At least I know they're still around," Smith took a long swig of beer. "That makes my situation more bearable. And I'm going to get them back home. I really messed up but I'm going to make sure I make things right."

"Just listen to us," Webber was now slurring his words. "If someone told me a few years ago I'd be having this conversation with you I would have had them committed on the spot."

"You're actually alright, Webber," Smith raised his glass in the air. "And I really enjoy working with you. And if you repeat that to anyone, I'll deny it emphatically."

"Fair enough," Webber smiled and lifted his own glass. "I really have to be going. I have to admit this has been rather enjoyable."
"Can I quote you on that?"
"Don't push it," Webber drained what was left in his glass. "I'll see you bright and early tomorrow."

* * *

A couple of miles away on the other side of the city a man was waiting. In the dimly lit room, he was waiting for his heartbeat to slow sufficiently to allow him to continue something he'd been planning for months.
Sixty-five beats per minute.
It was a healthy heart rate, but it was still too fast. He breathed in deeply a few times and looked at the watch on his wrist again.
Sixty-one.
He held out both hands in front of his face and looked at them for quite some time. He was sure the left hand was shaking slightly. Another quick glance at the sports watch told him it was almost time. His heart rate had slowed to fifty-five beats per minute.

He looked at the L96 sniper rifle safely secured in the stand in front of him. He unclipped the straps holding it in place and laid it carefully on the carpet. He'd cleaned it earlier and now the thirty-year-old rifle looked like new. He opened the case containing the Schmidt and Bender telescopic sight and, with a practised hand attached it to the L96. He then inserted the cartridges into the ten round magazine, even though he knew nine of those cartridges would be redundant.
The dial on his watch now read fifty beats per minute.

The man turned off the lamp and shuffled towards the window. It opened upwards a full ninety degrees to the frame. He instinctively got into position. He'd done it so many times before he did it without thinking. The barrel was resting on the window frame.

The thick clouds meant that visibility wasn't ideal, but it didn't matter. This moment had been practised so many times before, the man was sure he could carry it out blindfolded.

"Six floors up," he whispered. "Three squares to the right."

He glanced at his watch again.

It was almost time.

At nine-thirty on the dot, there was a movement in one of the windows on the top floor of the block of flats approximately six hundred metres away. The light was on in the third flat to the right. Through the 6 x 42 telescopic sight the woman came into the man's line of vision. He watched as she unrolled her yoga mat and placed it on the floor. After a few prayers she held out her arms and turned her palms upwards, her eyes closed the whole time.

With his finger placed gently around the trigger the man inched the L96 slightly to the right. The woman's forehead was now directly in the centre of the scope. Her eyes opened wide as though she could sense what was about to happen and before she had a chance to move, the man squeezed the trigger.

CHAPTER TEN

Smith arrived at the station before the rest of the team for once. He'd woken early and, after a cup of coffee decided to head straight to work. It was not yet seven in the morning. He nodded to the young PC manning the front desk and headed for the canteen. The place was deserted. Smith selected a coffee from the machine and sat at his usual table by the window. The clouds that had threatened rain during the night had drifted off to the west and the sky was now clear. He took out his phone and gazed at the photograph on the screen.

Whitton and Laura.

The photograph had been taken a few months earlier by Whitton's mum, Jane. It was a very good photo and both mother and daughter are smiling into the camera as though they'd just heard something funny. Smith wondered what they were both doing now, and he smiled when he realised exactly what Laura would be doing. She was an early riser and the first thing on her mind was always food. If she didn't get something inside her stomach within ten minutes of waking, she was grumpy for the rest of the day.

    Smith sensed a presence in the canteen and looked up from his phone. It was Yang Chu. The young DC looked tired.

"You're in early, Sarge," he said and sat down opposite Smith.

"I woke up early," Smith told him. "You look like you could do with a few more hours in bed."

"Toothache kept me up all night," Yang Chu explained.

"You should see a dentist."

"Really?" Yang Chu said sarcastically. "I tried to get an appointment but the earliest they could fit me in is Monday. Don't get a toothache on the weekend if you can help it. I've taken a couple of painkillers."

    Bridge came in with PC Baldwin. They were both laughing.

"What's so funny?" Yang Chu asked.

"You wouldn't get it," Bridge said.

He got some coffee for Baldwin and himself and they both sat down.

"What's up with you two?" Bridge asked Smith and Yang Chu. "You both look miserable."

"He's got a toothache," Smith pointed to Yang Chu. "And I'm just naturally miserable. You ought to know that by now."

"Where's Whitton?" Bridge said. "Everyone else is here but Whitton."

"How the hell should I know?" Smith said. "I'm going to check my emails." He stood up and left the canteen. His coffee was left unfinished.

"What?" Bridge said when he saw Yang Chu and Baldwin were both glaring at him.

"You should learn to think before you open your mouth," Yang Chu said and put his hand over his face.

His tooth was throbbing.

"I'm thinking about putting in for a transfer," Baldwin said.

"What for?" Bridge asked.

"What do you think? The atmosphere is unbearable at work. I thought it would get easier with time, but it hasn't."

"It'll blow over," Bridge said.

"I slept with Whitton's husband," Baldwin reminded him. "I spent the night with the husband of one of my best friends' and colleagues. That is something that doesn't just blow over."

"It was ages ago," Bridge wasn't giving up. "Besides, shit happens."

"Well I'm seriously considering applying for a transfer."

"Where to?" Yang Chu asked.

"Somewhere far away from here," Baldwin said. "Maybe somewhere down south."

"You won't last five minutes down south." Bridge said.

"What time is Webber's expert getting here?" Yang Chu changed the subject rather blatantly.

"Sometime this morning," Baldwin said.

"A woman gun expert," Bridge mused. "That's actually quite a scary thought."

"Why can't a woman be an expert in ballistics?"

"It's just not right somehow."

"You're such a sexist sometimes."

"I am not," Bridge protested. "I love women – I am certainly not sexist."

"I give up," Baldwin said shaking her head.

"You give up on what?" It was Chalmers.

The DCI had come in without them noticing. Whitton was standing next to him.

"I give up trying to understand what goes on inside Bridge's head," Baldwin told him.

"I gave up on that a long time ago," Chalmers laughed. "What's with the early start? Where's Smith?"

"He's in his office," Bridge answered Chalmers' second question first. "And it looks like none of us could sleep. We're all intrigued about this ballistics expert of Webbers'."

"Hmm," Chalmers said. "Any new developments in the shooting yesterday?"

"Nothing yet, sir," Yang Chu replied. "No witnesses and we still don't have an ID on the bloke."

"Someone must be missing him by now."

CHAPTER ELEVEN

Somebody was missing Charles Lincoln. His partner, Liam hadn't heard from Charles for almost twenty-four-hours. Liam had tried phoning him but each time the call went to voicemail.

"His phone battery probably died," Liam's friend Gavin suggested. "It happens."

"Not to Charles it doesn't," Liam said. "He will never let his battery drop below fifty percent. This isn't like him. Something's wrong."

"Don't jump to conclusions," Gavin said. "There's always a perfectly good explanation for everything."

"We were supposed to be going into town shopping today," Liam added. "If Charles couldn't make it, he would have phoned to let me know."

"Maybe he lost his phone," Gavin wasn't giving up.

In the end, Liam couldn't take it anymore. He'd known Charles Lincoln for eighteen months and they were even talking of moving in together. Charles was one of the most infuriating people Liam had ever met – with his pedantic tendencies and his inability to ever accept he may be in the wrong, but Liam had fallen head over heels for him. After the umpteenth time trying to get hold of Charles, Liam had jumped in his car and headed straight for York Police station.

It was just after eight when he approached the front desk. A man in a black T-Shirt and black jeans was talking to a man in uniform behind the desk.

"I need to report a missing person," Liam came straight to the point.

The uniformed policeman looked at him. From his name badge, Liam could see he was PC Fields.

"PC Fields," Liam said. "I haven't heard from my friend and I'm worried about him. It's not like him."

The man in jeans and T-Shirt appeared to find this information interesting. "DS Smith," Smith introduced himself. "When did you last see your friend?"
"Thursday evening, but I spoke to him on the phone yesterday morning."
"Technically," PC Fields interrupted. "A missing person is not missing until they've been missing for twenty-four-hours."
Liam looked at his watch. "Then my friend, Charles Lincoln is now officially missing. It is eight-fifteen now, and I last heard from him at ten past eight yesterday morning. And I haven't heard anything from him since. He's not answering his phone. It's not like Charles not to answer his phone."
"OK," Fields sighed. "Let's get the ball rolling then. There are some forms to fill in. If you could just take a seat, I'll find someone to come and speak to you."
"Something's not right," Liam said. "He told me he was going for a walk in the park and that's the last I ever heard from him."

Smith's ears pricked up. He had a feeling in his gut that the man in front of him was right – something was definitely wrong.
"Liam," he said. "Could you come with me please?"
"What's going on?" PC Fields asked.
Smith looked him in the eyes. "What you can do right now, PC Fields, is organise a couple of cups of coffee. We'll be in my office. Can you do that?"
Fields frowned. "Of course, sir."

"What's this all about?" Liam asked Smith in his office. "Do you know something?"
"This might be nothing," Smith said. "But I need to ask you a couple of questions. What time did Charles go to the park yesterday?"
"I told you, I spoke to him just before he set off. It was around ten past eight."
"And do you know what Charles was wearing yesterday?"
"What is going on here?" Liam raised his voice.

There was a knock on the door and PC Fields came in with two cups of coffee. He placed them on Smith's desk and left.

"Please just answer the question," Smith said. "Do you know what your friend was wearing yesterday when he went to the park?"

"Probably his full hiking attire," Liam laughed a very insincere laugh. "Charles has to do everything right. So, he was probably wearing the Helly Hanson boots he paid an absolute fortune for and his all-weather Musto jacket. Bright red. I've got a photo somewhere of him in his trekking gear." Liam fished out his phone and opened up his photographs.

"Here," he handed the phone to Smith.

It took Smith less than a few seconds to realise that the man in the photograph was now lying in the mortuary with half of the back of his head missing.

CHAPTER TWELVE

Helmand Province, Southern Afghanistan
A few years earlier

"How bad is it?" Lance Corporal Julie Ayres asked Staff Sergeant Moore. They'd dragged Private Darwin behind the RG. The armoured vehicle was still under heavy enemy fire. The whirring sound of aeroplanes could be heard in the distance.

"Looks like he took it in the shoulder," Moore was bent over Darwin and was trying to get a closer look.

Darwin's eyes were closed but he was breathing heavily.

"How are you doing, son?" Moore asked him.

Darwin opened his eyes and nodded.

"You're going to be alright," Moore added. "We'll get you out of here soon."

Private King was still busy picking off Taliban fighters on the mountainside opposite them.

The planes were getting louder now.

"About bloody time," Lieutenant Paul Jacobs looked up at the black sky then he looked at Moore. "How's he bearing up?"

"I can't see properly, sir," Moore replied. "But I think it went straight through his shoulder."

The planes were now directly overhead.

Then everything seemed to go quiet. The hum of the engines slowed and appeared to stop.

The first onslaught lit up the sky with a fierce display of orange, white and yellow. The explosions drowned out the sound of the gunfire. The second wave of planes arrived and once again the sky was lit up. The smoke engulfed the valley below.

The third line of fighter planes focused on the hilltops above the valley. The whole mountainside was subjected to a fierce attack and Private King put down his rifle. He knew he wouldn't need it anymore.

* * *

Private Tim Darwin was transported to a field hospital inside Camp Bastion. His prognosis was positive – the bullet had entered his left shoulder just above the clavicle and exited cleanly. He'd been lucky. A few millimetres higher and the bullet would have gone straight through his neck. He wasn't going to be firing a rifle any time soon, but he was expected to make a full recovery.

The valley in Musa Qala was still smouldering, days after the onslaught. General McNeill had considered the operation a huge success for the ISAF. Even though Afghani soldiers had been amongst the casualties the Taliban had retreated to higher ground and were busy contemplating their next move.

Darwin sat up higher in the hospital bed and winced at the pain in his shoulder.

"Do you want me to see if I can get them to give you something for the pain?" Private King asked.

"I want to feel it," Darwin winced again and took a deep breath. "I want to feel the pain, so I make sure I never get shot again."

"You're even more fucked in the head than me."

"Did we win?"

"What?" King asked.

"Please don't tell me I got shot and we didn't even win."

"We won," King said. "Apparently."

"What does that mean?"

"Mc Neill called it a major breakthrough," King sighed. "A huge step in overcoming the Taliban. They had to retreat to higher ground and McNeill reckons the ISAF will make sure they're forced to stay there for the duration of the winter. He thinks the cold will finish them off."

"You know that's not going to happen, don't you?"

"General McNeill seems confident."

"You'll see," Darwin said. "This is like Vietnam all over again. I read a book about it, and the American Generals thought the exact same thing. It is almost impossible to beat an enemy on their home turf."

"Like football you mean?"

Darwin laughed and felt a searing pain in his shoulder. "Something like that."

Neither of them said a word for a while. Darwin looked at Private King. "I saw the one who shot me you know."

King's eyes widened.

"I saw him when it was too late." Darwin added.

"Oh."

"He was dressed all in black – that's probably why he was so hard to see at first."

"I have to go," King said. "When do you think they'll let you out of here?"

"He didn't move," Darwin ignored his question. "But I saw him. Did you see him too?"

"I'll come back and see you when I can," King stood up. "It's quietened down a bit. The Yanks have taken over as usual. I'll see you soon."

Private Darwin closed his eyes and tried to ignore the pain in his shoulder. He'd been assured that the pain would ease after a week or so when the muscle tissue had healed. He thought about his wife back home. He was going to be a Dad. It almost didn't happen – his child was almost made fatherless before it was even born.

Then he thought about the moments before he was shot. He could remember every second of it – every sound and every smell. Private King and he had been firing off shots in quick succession.
Crack, crack, crack, crack.
Soon they formed a rhythm all of their own. In sync with one another.
Ten shots – reload then ten more.
The rifle fire from the other snipers in their convoy was blanked out.
    Darwin had stopped shooting.
So had Private King. Darwin remembered it clearly – King was no longer firing off shots. Then the man dressed in black appeared in his sights and Darwin prepared for the shot.
His chest began to burn, and he clenched his teeth when he realised something for certain. The man in black was clear as day now.
And Private King had seen him too.

CHAPTER THIRTEEN

"Let's get started, shall we?" Smith spoke to the rest of the team.
Bridge, Whitton, Yang Chu and Baldwin all looked at him expectantly.
"We have a possible lead on the man shot yesterday morning in Hove Park. Charles Lincoln. His friend came in earlier and reported him missing. Mr Lincoln's friend is yet to make a positive ID, but the timescale fits as does the description we were given so, until we have more to go on, we will assume the victim is Mr Lincoln. Any objections?"
"It's him," Yang Chu said. "He was wearing the exact same jacket as the one in the photograph."
Smith had made a copy of the photo on Liam's phone and everyone in the team had seen it.
"I agree," Whitton said. "It's far too much of a coincidence not to be him."
"Good," Smith said. "At least now we have something to go on. The ballistics report is going to take some time so until we have that we will concentrate all our efforts on finding out more about this Charles Lincoln man. He must have been targeted for a reason. You don't carry out such a sophisticated assassination on a random victim."
"Assassination?" Bridge repeated. "Do you think he was assassinated?"
"Do you think it's because of his name?" Yang Chu joined in. "Do you think someone with the surname Kennedy will be next?"
"Let's not get carried away," Smith said. "It was just a figure of speech."
   The door to the conference room opened and PC Fields came in.
"Sorry to interrupt, but I thought you'd want to know that the body has been identified as Charles Lincoln."
"Thanks, Fields," Smith said.
The young PC stayed where he was.
"Was there something else?" Smith asked him.

"My shift has finished, sir," Fields said.

"Then why are you still here?"

"And I'm not on duty anymore."

"That's usually what happens when your shift is finished," Smith was getting impatient. "What is it? Spit it out."

"I was just wondering if I could sit in on the meeting, sir. I won't say anything – I'll just listen. I want to be a detective someday. You won't even know I'm here."

"Why not?" Smith didn't want to waste any more time. "Sit at the back and keep quiet. Where were we?"

"Presidential assassinations," Yang Chu reminded him.

"This is not about assassinating people with the same name as murdered American presidents," Smith said. "Charles Lincoln. Like I said, we need to concentrate on finding out more about this man. Who was he? Look into his past and see if anything jumps out at you to indicate why someone would want to kill him. This was a well-planned murder – something about the man must shed some light on why he was killed like this."

"Is his friend up to questioning?" Whitton asked.

"Fields?" Smith looked at the young PC.

"He's rather distraught, sir, but I'm sure you'll agree that's quite normal under the circumstances. Distraught or not, I think time is of the essence and you shouldn't really put off interviewing a potential important witness based on his frame of mind. He may even be involved somehow."

Smith realised a smile had appeared on his face. Listening to PC Fields was like going back in time to when he started off as a PC.

It seemed like a million years ago now.

"Exactly," he said. "You're dead right there. Whitton, you and Yang Chu can speak to him. No offence, Bridge, but I think Whitton and Yang Chu will be able to handle the interview with slightly more sensitivity."

"None taken," Bridge said. "I completely agree with you."

Smith looked at his estranged wife. "Set it up."

The door to the conference room opened and Grant Webber came in. He was accompanied by a dark-haired woman who appeared to be in her late fifties. She was extremely short. Smith thought she couldn't have been more than four-feet-six. She was carrying a laptop computer.

"Good morning," Webber said. "Sorry we're late, but Gwen and I had a few things to go over."

"Are you the gun lady?" Bridge asked with his usual tact.

Gwen Culvert's face showed no emotion. "I've been called worse."

"Sorry," Webber said. "Everybody, this is Gwen Culvert. Gwen is an expert in the field of ballistics. Gwen, meet the team. DS Smith, DS Bridge, and DC's Whitton and Yang Chu."

He looked at PC Fields. "What's he doing here?"

"I said he could sit in," Smith said. "What have we got so far?"

"It's still early days," Gwen told him and removed her laptop from its case. "I need to link this up to the screen."

"I'll do it," Yang Chu offered.

He turned on the huge screen and connected the laptop. After a few seconds a large-scale map of York appeared.

"Just give me a few seconds," Gwen tapped away on the keyboard. "Good. That red star at the bottom is Hove Park. If I zoom in, we can see the exact spot where that poor gentleman was killed yesterday. There."

Smith was amazed. Even the small lake was visible on the screen.

"Right," Gwen continued. "Like I said, it's early days, but after collating a number of factors I can give you a provisional idea of where the rifle was fired from. The cartridge entered through the man's forehead and exited out the back of his head and lodged into a tree at a height of roughly one metre.

The victim wasn't a tall man – maybe one metre sixty, but we immediately know the shot was fired from above."

She continued to tap on the keyboard and the map on the screen changed. "What we see now is a topographical view of the city. It's basically a two-dimensional elevation profile view."

She stood up and approached the screen.

"This is the park," she pointed to the bottom right-hand corner. "And this black line is the estimated trajectory of the cartridge. York has very few high spots, and as you can see there are not many places where the black line makes contact with the skyline. Here, here and here."

She emphasised this last part by roughly stabbing at the screen with her index finger.

Smith stood up to take a closer look. "Do you know how far the bullet travelled before hitting its target?"

"No," Gwen replied.

"Not even a rough estimation?"

"Between three and six-hundred metres."

"So, it could have been fired from any one of these three places."

"Where are they?" Yang Chu had joined him in front of the screen.

"The first one is just behind Thief Lane," Smith said. "That one is a quarter of a mile away from the lake in the park as the crow flies."

"A cartridge from an L96 tends to fly as the crow flies," Gwen pointed out.

"There's a load of flats behind Thief Lane," Bridge joined in. "I bet that's where the shooter fired from."

Smith glared at him. "The second one is about fifty metres from there. Higher up of course."

"Wouldn't the flats obscure the view?" Whitton asked.

"Not according to this. There's a slight hill going up Lawrence Street. And the third one is just behind there."

"That shouldn't be too hard to check out," Yang Chu sounded optimistic.
"It's just a basic theory so far," Gwen said. "I'll be able to pinpoint it more accurately when I've spent a bit more time on it."
"This is enough to be going on with," Smith said. "At least we can start looking in the right places. Thank you, Mrs Culvert, you've been a great help."
"I'll keep you informed," she said. "I still have a lot to go through."

Smith and Bridge were about to leave the station when Baldwin approached them. She seemed very agitated.
"Can I have a word?" she asked Smith.
"Not now, Baldwin," Smith said. "We've got pressing matters to attend to."
"I think there's been another one."
"Another what?"
"Shooting," Baldwin said. "A man has just phoned in. He was quite hysterical, but he managed to calm down enough to tell me he found his wife dead in their flat."
"Get some uniform over there."
"He said he found her lying on the floor covered in blood. And half of her face had been blown off."

CHAPTER FOURTEEN

"Interview with Liam Riley commenced 11:30," Whitton said. "Present DC Whitton and DC Yang Chu. Mr Riley, how are you feeling?"

"Numb," Liam said. "Like this is all a dream and I'm waiting to wake up."

"Mr Riley," Whitton continued. "I realise this is extremely hard, but we need to move quickly. Would you like something to drink?"

"Not unless you have a bottle of vodka at hand. Sorry, no. Can we please just get it over with?"

"OK, this is not a formal interview and you are free to leave at any time. We're just trying to find out more about Mr Lincoln. How exactly do you know him?"

"He's my partner. We've been together for a year and a half."

"Your business partner?" Yang Chu asked.

"My *partner* partner. We were talking about getting a place together. Who on earth would do such a thing?"

"That's what we're going to find out," Whitton promised. "What did Mr Lincoln do for a living?"

Liam's top lip began to quiver, and he started to cry.

"Take your time," Whitton said.

"I'm sorry, it's just so much to take in. And you're already talking about him in the past tense. Would you mind if I didn't do that just yet?"

"Of course not. Go on."

"Charles is a graphic designer. He calls himself an artist, but he designs logos for various products. He's very good at it even though he's a bit of a perfection freak."

"What do you mean?" Yang Chu asked.

"He used to involve me in his work," Liam said. "And I'd always tell him the truth, and it was mostly positive. His work is excellent, but Charles always strived for more than that. *It has to be perfect*, he'd say."

"Can you think of anyone who would want to harm him?" Yang Chu asked.

"Of course not. He wouldn't hurt a fly."

"And you can't think of any recent arguments he's had with anyone?" Whitton said. "Anything at all?"

"Charles doesn't suffer fools, but he rarely argues. He'd rather avoid a person altogether than get into a confrontation. I'd quite like something to drink now if that's possible."

Yang Chu left the room and returned with a bottle of water.

"Interview with Liam Riley recommenced, 11:42," Whitton said. "Mr Riley, I have to ask you this. Where were you yesterday morning between 8 and 9 say?"

"Excuse me?"

"Please answer the question," Yang Chu pressed.

"You can't possibly think I had anything to do with this?"

"As far as we can see," Whitton said. "You were the person closest to him. Where were you yesterday morning?"

Liam thought for a moment. "Between eight and nine I was at home getting ready for work. I own a small second-hand book shop."

"Can anybody confirm this?"

"I live alone. I got ready for work and set off at around eight-forty-five. The shop is a fifteen-minute walk from my flat, and it was a nice day for a walk. I didn't hurt Charles."

"Nobody is saying you did," Yang Chu said and glanced at Whitton.

"Interview with Liam Riley ended, 11:45," Whitton said and switched off the recording device. "Mr Riley, is there anybody we can call for you? Family, friends?"

"I'll phone my friend, Gavin," he said. "He can come and pick me up. I'm going to have to tell Charles' mother. It's going to destroy her."
"Would you rather we did that for you?" Whitton offered. "We can contact his next of kin if you like."
"It's just Charles' mother. His scumbag father made it quite clear that Charles was no longer his son when he found out about us."
"I'm sorry," Whitton said.
"We will do everything we can to find out who did this to Charles," Yang Chu added.

* * *

Smith got out of his car and looked around. The address Baldwin had given him was in a part of York he'd never actually been to before. Three streets up from the river, it was part of a development that was barely a few years old. Three, six storey blocks of flats stood side by side. Below was a large parking space and a stretch of lawn that had clearly been planted very recently. Bare patches of grass had yet to grow.
"I didn't even know this estate existed," Smith said to Bridge.
"Don't let the residents hear you talk like that," Bridge laughed. "This isn't an *estate* – it's what's known as *luxury living*."
"If you say so. Webber's on his way, so I reckon we wait for him before we go in. The flat is on the top floor."
"Penthouse," Bridge corrected him.
"Have you recently subscribed to bloody Home and Garden or something?" Smith said. "I'm going to look around down here."
"What for?"
"I need to do some mental calculations."

He walked away without offering Bridge any further explanation. The dead woman was in the middle block. There were four large flats, or penthouses at the top. The woman lived in the third one from the right.

Smith stood directly in front of the building and turned his back to it. He could just make out the river behind the trees in the distance. He imagined the residents in the penthouses had to have impressive views from up there. Something was bothering him. Between the flats and the river there were two streets of houses and beyond the river he knew there were more new housing developments. There was money in this area of the city.
A lot of money.
Smith knew from past experience that when the well-fed entered into the equation, problems always seemed to follow.

"Webber's here," Bridge shouted. "And he's brought the gun midget with him."

CHAPTER FIFTEEN

"Where's the husband?" Smith asked the PC who'd met them inside as he, Bridge, Webber and Gwen Culvert entered the lift.
"He's with a friend in the next penthouse," he replied. "Sounds like he's in a bad way."
"He's my number one suspect right now."
"It's always the husband, isn't it?" Gwen Culvert said. "Isn't that what you lot always say?"
"No," Smith looked at her. "But it nearly always is."

The lift slowed and stopped silently. The doors opened out onto a large landing that was dotted with pot plants and small coffee tables and chairs.
"This is how the other half live," Bridge was clearly impressed.
"Not necessarily the better half," Smith scoffed.
"You're just jealous. I'd love to own a pad like this."
"Well I wouldn't. This is the place here."
Two more uniformed officers stood sentry outside the door.
"Has anyone else been inside?" Webber asked.
"No, sir," the taller of the two replied. "The woman's husband is next door. He's a total train wreck."
"When I need psychological insight, I'll seek the opinion of a shrink," Webber said and opened the door to the penthouse.

Smith followed him inside. The splendour of the landing was nothing compared to what met him in here. A two-metre high window ran the whole length of the main living space. He could see the River Ouse quite clearly down below. Pleasure boats were dotted all along its length. Smith had to admit that the view was truly breathtaking. The spires of the Minster were glowing in the early-afternoon sun, and the city beyond was framed by fields far, far in the distance.

"Wow," was all Bridge could manage.

Webber and Gwen Culvert got to work. The woman, whose identity had been confirmed as Diana Wells was lying on her back on a black rubber mat. The mat had been placed on the marble tiles.

"Christ," Webber said and turned away.

"Bloody hell," Bridge added.

The top half of Diana Wells' face was missing. Her forehead, both eyes and half of her nose were now a bloody mess. Her blonde hair was matted with black blood and bone pulp.

"Not a pretty sight," Gwen Culvert said calmly.

"What's that mat she's lying on?" Bridge asked.

"It's a Yoga mat," Webber replied.

"I didn't know you did Yoga."

"I don't, but Bryony used to be quite into it."

"Do you think it's the same killer?" Bridge said. "It looks like she was shot with a rocket launcher, not a rifle."

Gwen walked towards the huge window and crouched down.

"Find something?" Webber said.

"This is thick double glazing." She produced an odd-looking metal tool from her pocket and poked it through the hole she'd found in the glass. "Each pane is six-mil thick and it looks like there's a two-mil gap in between each pane."

"What does that mean?" Smith asked.

"I'm not sure. I've never seen anything like this before."

"Is it a bullet hole?" Bridge asked.

"Yes. That I am sure of, and if I'm not mistaken, from the thickness of the hole it made, we're looking at another very high calibre weapon."

She turned around and looked at the dead woman on the floor. Then she frowned.

"What's wrong?" Smith asked her.

"If what happened here is what I think happened, you've got a highly-skilled marksman on your hands."

"What do you mean?"

"We're in the penthouse of a six-storey building," Gwen said. "That would be hard enough, but to successfully shoot through two six mil panes of glass *and* hit the target is astonishing. I'm amazed that someone even attempted such a shot."

"We'll leave you to it," Smith said. "But there is one thing I don't understand."

"Go on." It was Webber.

"The man in the park had a hole the size of a two-pound coin in his forehead. If we're assuming this is the work of the same killer, why is half of this woman's face missing?"

"I think I can explain that," Gwen answered the question. "If I look at the window, I see two things. The size of the hole where the cartridge hit the window is much smaller than where it exited the other side."

"Why is that?"

"It's due to the two-mil gap in between the panes. The bullet hit the glass, and in doing so it changed its shape slightly, then for a fraction of a millisecond it passed through the gap between the panes but that was enough to increase its velocity. When it finally came out the other side, the shape of the cartridge was no longer pointed – the tip had been flattened and that's what did so much damage to that poor woman's face."

Smith shivered.

The faceless dead woman on the Yoga mat was starting to make him feel sick.

"Come on, Bridge, let's see if the husband is up to talking to us."

Smith stopped on the landing and took out his mobile phone. He'd thought of something. He brought up Whitton's number and called it.

"Hello," she answered quietly.

"Are you through with Liam Riley?" Smith asked her.

"It was a waste of time. I've lost count of how many times I've heard the phrases, *wouldn't hurt a fly*, and *I can't think of anyone who would want to hurt him*."

"Nothing then?"

"Nothing."

"I need you and Yang Chu to check out something. Webber's ballistics expert said something that got me thinking. She reckons the woman killed in the penthouse was shot by a very experienced marksman."

"My God."

"So, I want you and Yang Chu to find out about shooting clubs in and around York. Ask around – someone must know somebody capable of making such a difficult shot."

"I'll get onto it."

"Thanks," Smith said.

"What are you doing later?"

"Sorry?"

"Later," Whitton said. "Do you want to come round and see Laura?"

"Are you sure?"

"My mum and dad thought it might be nice for you to come round and have a bite to eat."

"I'll be there. Just tell me what time."

"At around six-thirty?"

"Perfect."

When Smith rang off he had a huge grin on his face.

"What's wrong with you?" Bridge asked him.

"Nothing," Smith lied.

"Rubbish. That look on your face is actually quite disturbing."

Six-thirty, Smith still had the grin on his face. At six-thirty he was going to sit down and eat with his wife and daughter for the first time in months.

CHAPTER SIXTEEN

Helmand Province, Southern Afghanistan
A few years earlier

"You lucky bastard," Lance Corporal Julie Ayres said in her broadest Glasgow accent. "You're going home."
"It took me almost dying for it to happen," Private Darwin said.
They both sat in the mess hall in Camp Bastian. Darwin rubbed his injured shoulder.
"It's lucky you're not left-handed," Ayres added. "At least you'll still be able to throw a ball around when the bairn gets older."
"I can't wait. Where's Private King? I haven't seen him for a while."
"He spends most of his time on the range now the action seems to have died down a bit. As if he's not a good enough sniper already."
"He wasn't so good back there in Musa Qala," Darwin said and frowned.
"What are you talking about? He picked off those Taliban like I've never seen anyone do before."
"He didn't get the one who shot me. The man in black. He must have seen him, and he did nothing."
"What are you trying to say, Private Darwin?"
"I'm saying that every time I think back, I come to the same conclusion – King waited for that Taliban sniper to shoot me."
"Easy," Ayres looked him directly in the eye. "That's quite a heavy accusation to be throwing around. It was a nightmare back there – there were shots coming from all over the place, and there's no way Private King would just sit back if he knew you were about to be shot."
"That's just what it looked like to me."
"You keep that opinion to yourself," Ayres said. "And that's an order."

Staff Sergeant Dean Moore came in. He nodded at Ayres and Darwin and headed for the food counter.

"Mind if I join you?" he asked and placed a plate of food on the table.

"Of course not, Sarge," Darwin looked at the mountain of scrambled eggs and bacon on the plate. "Is that for all of us?"

"Bugger off. This is all mine. Most important meal of the day, breakfast is."

"I can see that," Ayres laughed.

Moore tucked in.

"When are you leaving us?" he asked Darwin.

"Two days," Darwin told him. "I feel a bit bad about it to be honest. The shoulder is feeling much better now."

"I heard it won't be long before we'll be joining you," Moore said with a mouthful of bacon. "General Richards has had word from the Secretary of State that he's to pull half of the troops out. The Yanks have got it covered, and I for one agree with him. This is a battle nobody is going to win."

He placed his knife and fork on the empty plate and stretched his arms. "I'm going out to see if I can walk that lot off. Have you been down to the range recently?"

"Not since before I got shot," Darwin said. "I haven't really felt up to it."

"Do yourself a favour and get back on the horse. A talent like yours shouldn't be wasted."

"With respect, Sarge, I can't really see how being able to shoot a hole in a coin from a thousand yards is really going to help me back home."

"Join a club. There are plenty of gun clubs who would beg to have you on their team."

"I'll think about it."

"You do that," Moore said and stood up. "I'm off to see if there's any fresh air to be had around here. My stomach feels like there's a baby elephant living inside it."

"He's right you know," Lance Corporal Ayres said when Moore had gone. "There are loads of gun clubs who would kill for a deadeye like you."
"I don't think the wife would be too keen," Darwin said. "She hates guns."
"How far along is she now?" Ayres changed the subject.
"Six months. It's going to be a spring baby."
"You're going to have your work cut out for you. I've got some paperwork I need to get finished. Come and see me before you go."

* * *

Private Darwin could hear the sound of gunshots in the distance. Rifle shots.
The crack of the Arctic L96 was unmistakable. He walked towards the practice range and stopped behind the safety barrier. Private King was the only one practising today. He appeared to be concentrating hard and he didn't hear Darwin approach. Darwin watched as King went through the motions. He was aiming at a target six hundred metres away. His posture was different today. Darwin was always surprised when he watched King with a rifle in his hands. He seemed to be transformed into a different person. It was as though the rifle became a part of him. But today, his shoulders seemed tense and his eyes were darting from side to side.

Darwin waited for him to reload and approached from the back. "How's it going?"
King placed his L96 on the stand and turned around. "I'm having a bad day."
"Where's your spotter?"
"Welly? He's having a piss. The bloke's half-blind anyway – it's easier to do it myself. That bloke's not a spotter's arse. If you ask me, he shouldn't even be here."
Darwin picked up the spotting scope next to King. "Do you need a hand? I'll spot for you."

"Thanks," King said. "I'm way off with the 600, so I'll see if I can do any better with a quarter of a mile."

He finished reloading the rifle and moved into position. Darwin crouched next to him, adjusted the tripod of the spotting scope and focused it on the targets four-hundred metres away.

"Ready when you are."

King aimed and took the first shot.

"Eight to the left," Darwin said. "You are having a bad day."

King fired again.

"Same spot," Darwin said. "Try and relax your shoulders a bit."

"That's easier said than done," King said and fired off two shots in quick succession.

"Seven and eight," Darwin told him. "Both too low. What's going on?"

He knew that Private King could shoot consecutive tens on a 400m target with his eyes closed. This wasn't like him at all. King put down the rifle and sat up.

"My Wendy wants a divorce. I got a letter from her a while back and she wants a fucking divorce."

"I'm sorry," Darwin said.

"She's been shagging some other bloke. While I've been out here in this godforsaken place fighting for my country, my wife has been having it off with someone else."

He fired another shot.

"I don't know what to say," Darwin offered. "Is that why you've been acting a bit funny lately?"

"That's part of it."

"Take a couple of shots," King moved to the side and looked at Darwin. "It's been a while and I don't know if my shoulder is up to it yet."

"There's only one way to find out. Baby steps. Start with the 400. You can't do any worse than me."

Darwin decided to try. He crouched to the ground, rested the stock of the rifle on his good shoulder and looked through the sight.

"You said that's part of it," Darwin curled his finger round the trigger and squeezed.

"Six," King said. "Too high. What do you mean that's part of it?"

"You said just now that's part of it. What else is bothering you?"

He took another shot.

"Better," King said. "Eight to the right. This thing with Wendy has really been eating away at me. So much that it's been affecting my whole concentration. You were right. I did see that sniper dressed all in black at Musa Qala."

"You what?" Darwin could feel his heartbeat quickening.

"I saw him. It all happened so fast – I thought you had him and then he shot you. I'm sorry. It was my fault."

Darwin was silent. He focused on a white dot in the centre of the target and squeezed the trigger once more.

"Nine," King said. "Aren't you going to say anything?"

"What is there to say?" Darwin spoke to the rifle scope. "I don't blame you, especially now I understand the reason you weren't at full focus. Forget about it. I can't think of anything worse than finding out your wife has been cheating on you. Especially in a letter."

He squeezed the trigger once more. There was now only one cartridge left.

"Good," King said. "Nine. Right on the line. Between you and me, she's not going to get away with it. I've been thinking about nothing else since I read the letter and I've come up with the perfect way to make her pay."

Darwin had the centre of the target in his sight. "Go on."

"You have to promise never to repeat this to anybody," King said.

Darwin breathed deeply and his eyes narrowed. "I promise."

The shot echoed throughout the valley and Darwin put down the rifle.

"Ten," King shouted. "Right in the centre."

Then he told Private Darwin everything.

CHAPTER SEVENTEEN

Gordon Wells didn't even look up when Smith and Bridge came in. He was sitting next to an elderly woman on a huge leather sofa. Smith realised Wells' neighbours' penthouse was almost exactly the same as the one where Wells' wife was now lying dead. The window was the same height and length – the pillars dotted around the room were identical and even the walls had been painted the same off-brown colour.

The elderly woman got off the couch. "Come through to the dining room." She walked with surprising speed down a hallway without waiting for Smith to reply.

"I don't think he's going to be able to tell you anything yet," she said in the dining room. "Please take a seat."

Smith and Bridge sat down at the dark, wooden table.

"I'm afraid we need to speak to him urgently," Smith said. "Mrs?"

"James," she said. "Mrs James. But please call me Loretta."

"Loretta, we really do need to ask Mr Wells some questions."

"I appreciate that," she said. "But he's in a right state. It's shock, and I ought to know – I used to be a nurse."

"How long have you known the Wells?" Bridge asked.

"We moved in at the same time. Gordon and Diana and Olsen and I. As soon as the building work was finished as a matter of fact. It's taken quite a bit of work to get the place looking like it does today."

"Olsen James?" Smith thought out loud.

The name definitely rang a bell.

"That's right," Loretta said. "You'll no doubt have heard of him in your profession."

Now Smith remembered. Olsen James was once a Chief Constable. It was before Smith's time, but he remembered Chalmers mentioning the name a few times. James had been a force to be reckoned with if Smith remembered correctly.

"Gordon and Diana are a lovely couple," Loretta offered. "Olsen and I were a bit dubious at first – you know how young people can be these days, but they've been nothing but considerate since they moved in. They even warn us in advance of any social gatherings they may be planning."

"What did Mrs Wells do for a living?" Bridge asked.

"I don't think she worked. I could be wrong, but she very rarely left the penthouse. I think she was some kind of writer, but that's not really a proper job is it? This is all just awful. Do you know exactly what happened to her?"

"Not yet," Smith replied. "What about Mr Wells? Do you know where he worked?"

"He did tell me once, but it went straight over my head I'm afraid. Something to do with the Internet. He obviously does very well out of it. These places aren't cheap."

A groaning noise could be heard from the next room. It started off as a low, guttural growling then slowly rose in pitch until it was almost a wail. Smith and Bridge both shot up out of their chairs at the same time and went to see what it was. They found Gordon Wells crouched in the foetal position on the carpet. The sounds coming from his mouth were quite harrowing.

"I think I'd better call for a doctor," Loretta had come into the room. She looked at Smith and Bridge. "And I think you'd better leave."

* * *

Grant Webber was examining something on a large bookshelf against the wall in the Wells' penthouse when Smith and Bridge came back in. Gwen Culvert was nowhere to be seen.

"Find something?" Smith asked.

"It appears that Mrs Wells was a published author," Webber replied without turning around. "Crime thrillers. There are quite a few of her books here. They seem to have been produced by a reputable publisher too."

"I've never seen the attraction of crime thrillers," Bridge said. "They're nothing like what happens in real life."

"I didn't even know you could read," Webber said.

"Very funny. I happen to read quite a bit – I just don't like these unrealistic crime thrillers where the detectives are all alcohol-swigging womanisers."

Webber looked at Smith and smiled.

Smith smiled back.

"We didn't get anything out of the husband," he told the Head of Forensics. "He was screaming like a banshee when we left him. Mrs James, the neighbour is an ex-nurse and she's phoned for a doctor. You'll never guess who her husband is?"

"Amaze me."

"Olsen James."

"The ex-Chief Constable?" This made Webber turn around. "You're kidding?"

"Did you know him?"

"Only briefly. He retired shortly after I started. But I remember you didn't get on the wrong side of Olsen James if you could help it. How long do you think it'll be before Diana Wells' husband will be able to talk?"

"It's not looking promising," Smith admitted. "He's taken it very badly."

"Where's the gun lady?" Bridge asked.

"Will you stop calling her that," Webber snarled. "Show some respect. She's gone back to make a start on the prelim ballistics report. She found everything she needed."

"How soon can we move the body?" Smith asked.

He still couldn't bring himself to look at the mangled face of Diana Wells'.

"I'm nearly done. I'll let pathology know when I'm finished."

"Thanks, Webber," Smith said. "We'd better be getting back to the station. With any luck, Whitton and Yang Chu will have managed to find something out from the shooting clubs around here."

CHAPTER EIGHTEEN

Wendy Price suddenly remembered she'd forgotten to buy wine. In her shopping trolley she had all the ingredients for a perfect beef stroganoff – she'd also managed to find everything she needed according to the Pavlova recipe she'd found online, but it would all be ruined without a couple of nice bottles of wine to go with the meal.
Red for the main course and white for dessert.
She knew she would be out of luck finding the perfect accompaniment to her planned Russian evening – Russian wine wasn't something you came across every day, so she settled for the next best thing. She found the two most expensive Bulgarian wines on the shelf and added them to her trolley.

Wendy paid at the checkout using Dmitri's credit card and smiled when the acne-ridden youth working there didn't even glance at the name on the card. She put the credit card and receipt inside her purse, and she was still smiling as she pushed the trolley outside to the car park. It was late afternoon and the sun was high in the sky. The weather was perfect for what Wendy had planned – a few sundowners on the balcony looking onto the river, followed by a delicious meal.
And after that, who knew what would happen.

Wendy had met Dmitri Prici a few years earlier. He was in York attending a conference on renewable energy. At the time, Wendy worked as a receptionist at the hotel where the conference was being held. After her shift was over, she'd been in the bar having a few drinks with some work colleagues when she'd spotted Dmitri across the room. She remembered him sitting with some fellow conference delegates looking extremely bored. Wendy couldn't keep her eyes off him – he was older than her but something about the determination in his eyes fascinated her. She watched him for quite some time and when he got up to go to the bar, she made her move.

Wendy was immediately bewitched by this Russian with a passion for the environment. To her he was some kind of eco-warrior determined to save the planet. What Wendy didn't know at the time was that Dmitri's interest in renewable energy was driven by his majority share in a company that mass-produced solar panels in a factory in rural Russia. Dmitri Prici was in York to secure a deal that would earn him millions in the time it took to write a signature on a piece of paper.

Very soon, Wendy learned that Dmitri's interest in renewable energy had never been due to altruistic reasons, but by then she'd fallen head-over-heels in love with him. And the fact that he was wealthy beyond anything she'd ever imagined before seemed to lessen her own concerns for the environment. Dmitri's business deal was a roaring success and he remained in York to oversee the operations there. Wendy was happier than she'd ever been before. Her life was perfect. Dmitri even asked her to marry him.

There was only one problem.
At the time that Wendy met Dmitri, she was already married to another man. Rob King was a Private serving a term in Afghanistan. Wendy and Rob had been childhood sweethearts and marriage for them seemed like a natural progression. Rob joined the army and soon caught the eye of his superiors for his natural talent with a sniper rifle. To some he was one of the finest deadeyes they had ever seen, and with the conflict escalating in the Helmand district, it was inevitable that Rob would be sent to the heart of the war.

Wendy had a tough decision to make. Should she remain loyal to her childhood love or accept the proposal of the most enigmatic man she had ever met? She chose the latter. Rob King had little choice but to agree to the divorce and no sooner was it finalised that Wendy and Dmitri became man and wife. Deciding the name Prici could possibly hinder him in his new country of residence, Dmitri had it changed to a more English, *Price*, and Wendy King became Wendy Price.

Wendy opened the boot of her car and carefully placed her shopping inside. The smile was still on her face when she gazed up at the cloudless sky. A young mother was fighting a losing battle with a toddler in the car parked next to her. The young girl was refusing to get into the child seat in the back of the car.

Not my problem, Wendy thought.

This was going to be the perfect Sunday evening.

She was still smiling at the sky when her whole head exploded. The bullet pierced her left temple, cut its way through her brain and made its exit through the temple on the other side.

Wendy Price was already dead before she fell to the ground next to the open-mouthed mother of the stubborn toddler.

* * *

Just under a kilometre away a man in a black hatchback rolled up the window in the back of the car and covered up the modified Arctic L96 with a thick plastic sheet. He remained in the back seat until his breathing had returned to normal and then he opened the back door. The sun was still beating down over the city. He checked his heartbeat once more. It wasn't quite right, but he knew he had to get away from the car park as soon as possible. Apart from his car it was deserted but that could soon change. The derelict ground around the old industrial estate was notorious for its dubious nocturnal activities. He opened up the driver's side door and got inside.

This had been the third one, but the man knew this was the pivotal one. He could feel it. Everything was going to change once what had happened to Wendy Price was discovered. The first two had been leading up to this one but this was the one that would send them running off in all directions with no idea where they were heading.

CHAPTER NINETEEN

Smith and Bridge arrived back at the station just after five. Considering two people had been brutally murdered recently the station was eerily quiet. Baldwin wasn't behind the front desk. A man Smith had never seen before was talking on the phone.
Where do these people come from? He thought.
It seemed that not a day went by without some new face appearing at the front desk. He waited for the PC to finish his phone call.
"Have you seen Whitton and Yang Chu?"
"Who?"
"DC Whitton and DC Yang Chu," Smith elaborated. "Do you know if they're still here?"
"I'm new," the PC offered by way of an explanation.
"I can see that."
Smith shook his head and walked off in the direction of the canteen. Bridge followed him.

The canteen in the York police station was very close to achieving legendary status. It was in here that countless crimes had been cracked. Nobody knew what it was about the place – whether it was the relaxed atmosphere or the inspirational view from the window, but very often after weeks of getting nowhere in an investigation it was within the four walls of the canteen where the final pieces of the puzzle were put together. When Smith walked in today, he knew straight away that today was not going to be one of those days. The place was deserted. Smith was exhausted. It wasn't just the recent shootings that had taken their toll on him – the past couple of months after his separation from Whitton had been extremely stressful.

"Do you want coffee?" he asked Bridge.

"I could do with something much stronger," Bridge replied. "But coffee will have to do in the meantime."

Smith got them both a strong coffee from the machine and they sat down at their usual table by the window.

"Smyth's nephew is starting tomorrow," Bridge reminded Smith.

"Thanks," Smith took a sip of his coffee. "I didn't think things could get any worse around here."

"I wonder what he's like."

"Chalmers reckons he's nothing like the Super, but I can't see it myself. The Smyth name is synonymous with idiocy. He's bound to be a buffoon like his Uncle Jeremy."

"I wonder where Whitton and Yang Chu are," Bridge said. "And Baldwin for that matter."

"Probably gone home. To be honest, I don't blame them."

"We're in the middle of a double murder investigation."

"And we're playing the waiting game as usual," Smith sighed. "We're waiting for forensics and we're waiting to see what pathology can come up with. And now we have the pleasure of ballistics to wait for as well, not to mention relatives of the victims who all seem to be one step away from the nut house. We spend half our lives waiting in this place."

"You're getting cynical in your old age."

"I won't disagree with you there."

"And you're almost starting to sound like a true Yorkshireman." Bridge added.

Smith gazed out of the window. There was no indication that a change in the weather was on the cards – the sun was still blazing and the only clouds in the sky were small, fluffy, insignificant ones.

"Whitton's invited me round to her parents for a meal this evening," he told Bridge.

"That's brilliant," Bridge said. "Are you two getting back together?"

"It's still early days, and it was her parents' idea, but it's a start. I miss her and Laura like you wouldn't believe. Speaking of which, I forgot to ask her if I needed to bring anything."

He took out his phone. The screen was blank. He tried switching it on, but nothing happened.

"Shit, the battery must have died."

"Use mine," Bridge rummaged in his pocket and frowned. "I must have left it somewhere."

"I'll phone her from the front desk."

They went down together. The clueless PC was nowhere to be seen. Lights were flashing on and off on the small switchboard behind the desk. "That idiot isn't going to last long around here with his attitude." Smith said and picked up the handset next to the switchboard. "Or maybe he will."

He keyed in Whitton's number and waited. She answered almost immediately.

"DC Whitton."

"It's me," Smith told her. "My phone battery must have died. Where are you?"

"We've been trying to get hold of you for ages," Whitton told him.

"I told you, my battery died."

"What about Bridge? He's not answering his phone either."

"He can't find it. What's going on?"

"A woman was shot earlier in the car park of the supermarket off Jenkins Road. It looks like another sniper attack. Half of her head is gone."

* * *

Smith and Bridge made it to Jenkins Road in less than five minutes. The supermarket was one Smith had shopped at many times before. He got out of his car and walked towards the obvious crime scene. A wide area had already been cordoned off with police tape and four police cars with their lights flashing were parked in front of it. An ambulance with the back door wide open was parked close to them. Smith spotted Webber and walked over. The Head of Forensics looked like he was about to keel over. His face was deathly pale, and he looked like he hadn't slept in weeks.

"Do you think it's the same gunman?" Smith came straight to the point.

"God, I hope so," Webber replied. "Because if there's more than one person in York doing this, we're in serious trouble. The woman's practically had her head blown off."

"Jesus," Smith said. "What have we got so far? Any witnesses?"

"Whitton and Yang Chu have spoken to a few people who were milling around when it happened, but if it's the same MO as the others, there's a high probability the gunman was far away when he pulled the trigger. A woman was putting her baby in the car seat next to the dead woman's car when it happened. She's still in shock."

"Another one," Smith said.

"What?"

"Nothing. Do we have any idea who the dead woman is?"

"Wendy Price," Webber said. "Her driving licence was in her purse."

"This is really starting to get disturbing," Smith looked around the car park. Besides the police vehicles and the ambulance, there were very few cars left. He looked up and spotted something.

"Are those CCTV Cameras?" he asked Webber.

"Looks like it," Webber said.

"We need to see the footage."

"What for? That footage will give us as much as the witnesses if it's the same bloke."

"Think, Webber," Smith said. "If those cameras have filmed the woman being killed, we'll have a hell of a lot more for your ballistics expert to go on."

"I'm knackered," Webber said. "You're right. I should have thought of that."

"Get your team to go over the scene," Smith told him. "Delegate. You do not have to personally take over every crime scene in York. It's going to kill you if you carry on like this."

"I could say the same about you, but thanks. I'll do that."

"The supermarket doesn't close for another hour," Bridge said. "I'll go and see if the CCTV was operational."

Whitton and Yang Chu approached.

"Sorry it took us so long to get here," Smith decided to get in first.

"There's nothing you could have done anyway," Yang Chu sighed. "How are we supposed to catch a murderer who kills people without even being at the crime scene?"

"What do you think?" Smith said.

"Motive?"

"You and your bloody motive theory," Whitton said. "What possible motive could someone have for killing three people who, as far as we know, didn't even know each other?"

"Random sicko?" Yang Chu suggested.

"I don't think so," Smith said. "This isn't the work of a deranged mind – all this has been carefully planned in advance."

"I don't know," Yang Chu still wasn't convinced. "What if it's just some bloke with a rifle who's picking off victims when the opportunity comes along?"

"I sincerely hope not," Whitton said. "Because if that's the case we'll never catch him."

"There has to be a motive for all this," Smith was adamant. "There always is. There is always a common denominator with the victims. Always."

A car pulled up and parked behind the ambulance. DCI Chalmers got out of the passenger side. Shortly afterwards a man Smith had never seen before got out of the other side. He was short and stocky, and he walked with his head high. He was either very sure of himself or merely incredibly proud, Smith couldn't figure out which. Chalmers and the mystery man walked over to them.

"What are you doing here, boss?" Smith asked Chalmers.

"Everyone," Chalmers ignored his question. "The new DI was due to start work tomorrow but in light of what's happened recently, he insisted on having a look at the latest crime scene. May I introduce you all to Detective Inspector Oliver Smyth."

CHAPTER TWENTY

Harold Whitton opened the door with a smile.
"Come in, son," he held out his hand to Smith.
Smith shook it. "Thanks for inviting me. I didn't know what to bring, so I just picked up a few beers on the way."
"That'll do nicely. Jane's cooking us a nice gammon. I hope you're hungry."
Smith realised that he was. He hadn't eaten all day. He followed Whitton's Dad through to the kitchen. Whitton was sitting at the table with her mum.
"Hello," Jane's tone wasn't as friendly as Harold's.
She still hadn't forgiven Smith for what he'd done, and Smith knew it was going to take a long time to get back to how things used to be between them.
Harold opened two of the beers Smith had brought and put the rest in the fridge. He handed one to Smith.
"Cheers. I believe it's been a rough few days at work, what with the sniper attacks and everything."
"I told him," Whitton explained.
"It still doesn't seem real," Smith said and took a long swig of beer. "This sort of thing just doesn't happen in York. Where's Laura?"
"She's sleeping upstairs," Jane told him.
"Can I go and see her?"
"She's sleeping," Jane said coldly.
"I won't wake her up – I just want to look at her."
"It's alright, Mum," Whitton said and nodded to Smith.

   Laura was sleeping in the spare bed. Her mouth was open, and she was snoring softly. Smith bent down and kissed her gently on the forehead. He rested his nose in her hair and took in her scent. He breathed in deeply. He never tired of that scent – it was the smell of innocence. He breathed in a few more times and then he wasn't quite sure what happened. He felt a twitch in his face underneath his left eye – it spread to his mouth and then the tears came. He moved away from the bed and just sobbed. He tried to get the tears to stop but he couldn't. He waited until there were no more tears to shed, wiped his eyes and sat with his hands over his face.

"Are you alright?" Whitton had come inside the room.

"Not really," Smith admitted.

"The food's nearly ready. About five minutes."

"I'll come down in a minute," Smith wiped his eyes once more.

Whitton looked at him and smiled. Smith realised that she hadn't smiled at him in a very long time, and in that moment, he made up his mind that nothing else mattered. Everything he needed in his life was right there in that room. Everything else was totally insignificant.

"I'm just a bit knackered," he said after a few seconds.

"You smelled her hair didn't you?" Whitton asked.

"Am I that predictable?"

"Not always, but most of the time."

"Are we alright?"

"I don't know," Whitton looked away. "I honestly don't know."

"I don't give a shit about anything else. All I want is you and Laura and I'll do anything you ask to make that happen."

"I need some more time," Whitton told him. "Come on, the food's almost ready. Splash some water on your face – your eyes are all red and puffy."

"This is delicious, Mrs Whitton," Smith said and took another mouthful of food.

"When was the last time you ate anything?" Harold asked. "My Jane's food is good, but I've never seen anyone eat so much."

"It's been a long day," Smith said. "And I forgot to eat."

"Well, I'm stuffed," Harold said. "I'll leave you and Erica in peace and go and help Jane with the dishes."

"What did you think of the Super's nephew?" Whitton asked.

Smith put his knife and fork down on his plate. "It's hard to tell, but it's quite clear he's nothing like Smyth. He seemed quite confident and the Smyth gormless grin seems to have passed him by. I suppose we'll see tomorrow."

"Can you remember when Brownhill first arrived?"

"Brownhill didn't *arrive*," Smith said. "Brownhill exploded into the station. *Do I have to point out to you that you are a representative of the York Police department?*" Whitton said in a deep voice. "*And as such, the way in which you dress directly reflects upon us.*"

Smith started to laugh. "I really miss her you know."

"Me too. She was hard work at first, but she soon got to understand how we worked. I wonder if this Oliver Smyth bloke is going to come in and try and stamp his authority. On the other hand maybe it won't be such a bad thing if he does."

"What are you talking about?"

"Since Brownhill was killed there's something missing. There's no real leadership within the team."

"Thanks a lot," Smith said.

"I didn't mean you. It's clear that you're in charge of the investigations, but you're not exactly the authoritarian type. We all respect your decisions but you're more of a mate than a boss."

"So, I'm your mate at least?"

"Don't push it."

Harold Whitton came back in with two beers. He handed one to Smith. "There's a film on I've been wanting to watch. You're welcome to join us."

"What film is it?" Whitton asked.

"American Sniper. I know it's a bit close to home at the moment, but I've been wanting to watch it for a while now."

"I think I'll pass, Harold," Smith said.

"Dad's always been interested in stuff like that," Whitton explained. "It amazes me how someone can hit the target from so far away. That must take some practice."

"That reminds me," Smith said to Whitton. "Did you come up with anything at the shooting clubs?"

"We got hold of the owner of the biggest one," Whitton said. "He's agreed to speak to us tomorrow."

"Speaking of tomorrow," Smith downed his beer in one go. "I'd better be off."

He thanked Whitton's Mum for the meal and said goodbye to Harold.

"I'll see you tomorrow then," he said to Whitton on the doorstep.

"Bright and early. I'm intrigued to see what Smyth junior is like."

"Please don't call him that. I'll see you tomorrow."

Smith was about to leave when Whitton leaned closer and kissed him on the cheek. Smith turned around and walked up the road. The smile on his face stayed there all the way home.

CHAPTER TWENTY ONE

"The first thing I want to say is I'm honoured to be a part of this team." Detective Inspector Oliver Smyth's opening words surprised everyone. The new DI had gathered everyone in the small conference room at the station in order to introduce himself. Smith, Whitton, Bridge, Yang Chu and PC Baldwin were all seated, eager to hear what Superintendent Smyth's nephew had to say. DCI Bob Chalmers was also there.

Smith rubbed his temples. He'd woken up with a terrible headache and as the morning progressed it had got steadily worse.

"York Police has gained a reputation," Oliver continued. "And that reputation is well deserved. I believe in the whole of the UK, only Oxford has achieved the one-hundred percent clear up rate in murder investigations that York has and that is definitely something to be proud of. I appreciate that my posting here was due to tragic circumstances, but I assure you I will do my utmost to honour my predecessor."

Smith found himself nodding his head and this did nothing to relieve the pain which was now becoming unbearable. Even so, he had to admit this wasn't at all what he'd expected from the new DI.

"Let me introduce myself," Oliver carried on. "And give you a bit of info about what brought me here. I spent ten years in the armed forces in a special advisory position. I served terms in both Iraq and Afghanistan, and the nature of that position dictates that I've already said too much."

Smith started to laugh. DI Smyth stared at him. His expression was neither hostile nor friendly, but Smith composed himself.

"When I left the armed forces, I joined the police," DI Smyth said. "Firstly, in Newcastle then in Manchester. Big cities with big city problems. But when the DI post became vacant in York I jumped at the chance, and do you know why?"

Nobody spoke.

"Because I was curious how the police force in this historical town has cleared up every single murder on its doorstep."

"That's not quite true," Smith spoke for the first time.

"Excuse me?"

"DS Smith," Smith said.

"I know exactly who you are."

"We have three unsolved murders at the moment," Smith informed him.

"I am well aware of that," DI Smyth said. "But it's early days and I have every confidence in this team maintaining its one-hundred percent clear-up rate. Any questions?"

Smith nodded. "Are you going to restructure the team in any way?"

"As I see it," DI Smyth said. "I have no way of knowing the answer to that question until I've observed the dynamic of the team."

"But you'll be heading up any investigation from now on?" Smith continued.

"I believe that goes without saying. Does anybody have a problem with that?"

The pain in Smith's head was now excruciating and he was seeing flashes of light in front of his eyes.

"As I see it," he said. "I have no way of knowing the answer to that question until I've seen you in action."

"Very well. Any more questions?"

"Will you be getting your hands dirty?" Smith's vision was now becoming blurred. "Or will you lead from the comfort of your office."

Smith was unaware that Chalmers was glaring at him.

"I assure you," DI Smyth said calmly. "I am extremely hands-on. I believe in leading by example and my interrogation experience in military intelligence has taught me how to spot a liar from a thousand feet away."

"Isn't that an oxymoron?" Smith was now feeling quite sick.

"Excuse me?"

"Military intelligence," Smith said. "It's a famous oxymoron. It's a bit like Scottish cuisine."

"Very good. Now, if there's nothing else, I'd like to get up to speed with the developments in this sniper investigation. Smith?"

Smith didn't know what was happening to him. The vision in his right eye had now gone and all he could see out of his left eye was a white line that seemed to shimmer. He tried to blink it away but it only made it worse. He could feel his heartbeat throbbing in his head.

"Smith?" DI Smyth said once more.

Smith felt his head lean forwards. He shook himself awake but his eyelids drooped, there was a flash of light, and he couldn't stop his head from falling onto the table in front of him.

"Smith?" DI Smyth said once more.

Smith was still slumped over the table.

"What's wrong with him?" Bridge asked.

"Looks like he's fallen asleep," Yang Chu said.

"He's not asleep," Whitton stood up and walked over to Smith. "Something's wrong."

She tried to shake him awake but he didn't stir.

"Jason," she said. "Jason."

* * *

"Jason," the voice sounded like it came from somewhere miles away. Smith opened his eyes and winced at the bright light. He had a dull pain in his forehead just above his left eye.

"Jason," Whitton said once more. "How are you feeling? You gave us a real fright back there."

"What happened?" Smith asked her.

The last thing he remembered was DI Smyth's deep voice.

"You passed out in the conference room," Whitton told him.

"My head is throbbing," Smith said. "Why did I pass out?"

"They're not sure yet – they've done some tests and we'll know what's wrong soon."

"I feel terrible. It's an effort to even move."

A middle-aged doctor came in. He was holding a folder in his hand.

"How are you feeling?" he asked Smith. "I'm Doctor Frank Barnes."

"I've been better," Smith replied. "What's wrong with me?"

"We're not sure – the results of the CT and MRI scans didn't show up anything out of the ordinary so we can rule out any brain anomalies. Can you remember anything about what happened?"

"All I remember is talking to my DI," Smith said. "I woke up with a terrible headache this morning and it just seemed to get worse. The vision disappeared in my right eye and all I could see out of my left one was some sort of shimmering light. Then I woke up in here."

"Classic migraine," Dr Barnes said. "And a very severe one at that. Have you suffered from migraines in the past?"

"No. Nothing like this has ever happened before. Am I going to be alright?"

"I don't see why not. Did you experience the aura?"

"The what?" Smith was confused.

"An aura in your vision?"

"The shimmering light you mean?"

"Some people see flashing lights and others experience something similar to a kaleidoscope effect."

"It was something like that," Smith said. "What causes it?"

"I'm afraid we don't know exactly. Classic migraines are extremely rare, and losing consciousness during an attack is rarer still, but what we do know is they often follow periods of extreme stress."

"I'm not stressed," Smith said. "In fact my life is actually starting to get back on track."
He smiled at Whitton and the throbbing in his head got stronger.
"Many migraine attacks occur after the stress is over," Dr Barnes explained. "When the mind is at rest and able to contemplate what has just happened."
"Is there anything I can do about it?"
"I'm afraid we can't actually cure it. At this stage I would advise you to always have some pain killers at hand. We'll begin with pain-relief measures. You'll soon start to recognise the warning signs of an oncoming attack and quite often one is able to nip the pain in the bud before it becomes a full-scale migraine. If you start experiencing migraines on a regular basis, we can look at a more preventive approach."

"When can I go home?" Smith asked.
He was still trying to process what the doctor had just explained to him.
"I don't see any reason why you can't be discharged tomorrow morning," Dr Barnes said. "I'd like to keep you here overnight just to keep an eye on you – as I said loss of consciousness during a migraine attack is extremely rare, and not something to take lightly. But very often the first attack is the most severe, and I believe it is highly unlikely you'll experience such an attack in the future, especially once you begin to recognise the warning signs."
Smith sighed. He hated hospitals.
"I'll come and see you after work this evening," Whitton told him. "I'll bring Laura with me."
"Let me know how the investigation is going," Smith said.
"I'd better get back," Whitton leaned over and kissed him on the top of the head.

CHAPTER TWENTY TWO

The Greyham Rifle and Pistol Club was located a couple of miles outside of the city centre.

"How's Smith doing?" Bridge asked Whitton

"He's going to be fine," she said. "He suffered a severe migraine."

"He passed out because of a headache?"

"It wasn't just a headache – migraines can be quite debilitating. They're keeping him in overnight for observation."

"I bet he took that well."

"He did, funnily enough. I think he got a bit of a fright."

"What made him have the migraine?" Bridge said.

"Apparently they're not certain what causes them but relaxing after periods of stress can trigger them."

"Are you two getting back together?" Bridge changed the subject. "He misses you and Laura like mad you know."

"I don't know. I still can't forget what he did to me. And Laura too. This is the place here."

Bridge turned left and followed a gravel road for another few hundred metres. He drove through the gates of the grounds and followed the signs to the reception building. He parked his car outside, and he and Whitton got out. Yang Chu had drawn the short straw and had the dubious pleasure of accompanying DI Smyth to the workplace of the husband of the most recent sniper victim.

"I didn't even know this place existed," Whitton said.

They reached the entrance and went inside. The reception area was light and airy. Various photographs of what appeared to be shooting competitions hung on the walls.

"Can I help you?" the man sitting behind the desk asked them.

"We're looking for Billy Forest," Whitton told him. "We're from York police and Mr Forest agreed to speak to us yesterday."

"That'll be me," Billy stood up and held out his hand. "You don't mind if we go outside, do you? I feel like a bit of fresh air."

"It's just terrible what's happened," Billy said.

He, Whitton and Bridge were seated at a wooden bench overlooking the shooting ranges.

"I read about it in the papers," he added.

"That's why we're here," Whitton said. "We believe these shootings are the work of a highly-skilled marksman."

"Are you implying that one of the members of the GRPC is involved?"

"We don't know," Bridge admitted. "But we thought you might be able to help us with some names of experienced shooters."

"I can assure you that none of my members are responsible for these atrocities," Billy said. "This is a sports club – we do not make a habit of shooting people."

"We're not implying anything of the sort, Mr Forest," Whitton said. "We have three dead people, all of whom were shot at long range with a high-calibre rifle."

"Do you know what rifle was used?" Billy asked.

"It was an Arctic L96," Whitton knew it was only a matter of time before the press got wind of this information anyway.

Billy's eyes widened. "An L96?"

"That's right," Bridge said. "Do any of the members of your club use one of those on the range?"

"Of course not. You're talking about a military-issue sniper rifle. I'm not even sure if they're available to the general public."

"Well somebody has managed to get their hands on one," Bridge said. "And not only that, they know how to use it."

"One of the victims was shot in her sixth-floor penthouse," Whitton elaborated. "The shot penetrated two six-millimetre panes of glass and hit her in the head."

"That's quite a shot," Billy said.

"Are you aware of anybody who is capable of making such a shot?" Bridge asked.

Billy scratched his ear. "We've got some talented marksmen here. Do you know how far away the gunman was from the target?"

"We can't be sure, but somewhere in the region of six-hundred metres."

"My goodness."

"Are any of your members capable of such a shot?" Bridge was getting irritated.

"A few," Billy said. "But as I said, there is no way they would even contemplate shooting somebody in cold blood."

"Do you have their contact details?" Whitton asked.

"Of course," Billy said. "But they're not going to be too happy about being quizzed by the police."

"I'm afraid that can't be helped," Bridge said. "Could we have those contact details please?"

* * *

Yang Chu and DI Smyth drove in silence to the warehouse Price Solar operated out of. Yang Chu couldn't think of anything to talk about and it was clear from the expression on DI Smyth's face that he was not one for whom awkward silences posed a problem.

"This is the worst part of the job," DI Smyth eventually broke the silence. "Informing a husband or wife that their spouse is no longer alive. Unfortunately, it *is* a part of the job and we just have to get used to it. I'll do the talking if you don't mind."

"Of course." Yang Chu didn't mind at all.

They were directed by the receptionist to Dmitri Price's office and DI Smyth knocked on the door.

"Enter," a loud voice was heard on the other side.

They went inside and Yang Chu closed the door behind him.

Dmitri Price was seated behind a huge wooden desk. He was a broad-shouldered, dark-haired man and the bluish-black stubble on his face suggested he needed to shave at least once a day.

"What can I do for you?" he asked with a slight hint of an accent.

"Mr Price," DI Smyth said. "May we sit down?"

Price gestured to the two chairs facing his desk. Yang Chu and DI Smyth sat down.

"Mr Price," Smyth said. "We're from York CID."

"I can assure you that my business is all above board," Price looked at the DI suspiciously.

"That's not why we're here," DI Smyth continued. "I'm afraid we are here with very bad news. There was a shooting incident in town yesterday. And I'm afraid your wife was involved. The shooting was fatal."

"Wendy?" Price frowned. "What has Wendy got to do with some shooting incident?"

"She was shot, Mr Price," DI Smyth informed him. "I'm sorry, but Wendy is dead."

The silence that followed seemed to last forever for Yang Chu. He watched as Dmitri Price appeared to be digesting what DI Smyth had just told him.

"Are you sure?" he said eventually.

"Yes," DI Smyth replied. "Her driving licence confirmed it. When was the last time you spoke to your wife?"

"Yesterday evening. Around seven. She was planning on making a special supper and I had to let her know I wasn't going to be able to make it."

"Why is that?"

"Because I got delayed. I can't believe Wendy is dead."

"Is there anybody you would like us to call?" DI Smyth asked.

"Who shot her?" Price asked.

"Sorry?" His reply had obviously taken the DI by surprise.

"Who shot her?"

"We don't know that. I understand this must come as quite a shock, but we need to ask you a few questions. Is there someone you'd like us to call? Someone who can be with you while we talk to you?"

"Do I need a lawyer?"

"Of course not."

"But you think I'm involved somehow?" Price asked.

"We need to explore all avenues, Mr Price," DI Smyth told him. "Where were you yesterday afternoon? Between five and six?"

"I was out of town," Price said.

"Can anybody corroborate that?"

"Of course. My driver can confirm I was in London until this morning. As can roughly a hundred conference delegates."

"We'll check. Can you think of anybody who would want to harm your wife?"

"Of course not. Everybody liked Wendy. Who could possibly want to shoot her?"

"We're going to find out."

CHAPTER TWENTY THREE

"Eeny, meeny, miny, moe," the words sounded ridiculous coming from the mouth of a man holding an Arctic L96 sniper rifle.
"Catch a tiger by the toe."
From his vantage point he could see almost the whole of Gillygate. People were coming and going – all of them oblivious to the fact that one of them was going to be dead in roughly three minutes' time.
"If he hollers, let him go."
A very large woman was now in the centre of the telescopic scope.
"Too easy."
He shifted the rifle slightly to the right and focused on a more challenging target. A thin young man wearing a baseball cap was clearly up to no good. The modified scope meant the deadeye could see the malicious intent in his eyes. This man was clearly not just out for a morning stroll. The deadeye followed the thin man's progress as he made his way in the direction of the Minster. The expression in his eyes changed. He'd seen a potential victim and the hunt had begun.
The hunter was about to become the hunted.
 The deadeye checked his heartbeat.
Fifty-two beats per minutes. It was almost perfect. He curved his hand around the trigger and remained absolutely still. The potential thief's head filled the scope.
"Eeny, meeny, miny, moe."
With the last word, the deadeye squeezed the trigger and watched through the scope as the thin man's baseball hat came away from his head along with half of his brain.

* * *

"Mr Price," DI Smyth said. "I realise this is hard, but I need you to think hard about who could possibly have done this to your wife."

"I told you," Price said. "I have no idea. Wendy had no enemies as far as I am aware."

"What about you?" Yang Chu joined in. "Is there a possibility that somebody may have done this to get at you?"

Price glared at him. "Constable, I am a businessman – I deal in solar energy, and although it is a ruthless industry to be a part of, I can assure you we do not go around killing people. Just because I am Russian doesn't mean I am involved in Mafia dealings."

"I actually didn't know you were Russian," Yang Chu said. "Your English is excellent."

"Wendy was shot in broad daylight in a supermarket car park," DI Smyth decided on a different approach. "There were other people around at the time. It was a blatant shooting and in my experience that usually means whoever did this wanted to make a point."

"If she was shot in front of people then someone must have seen the person who did it," Price said. "Haven't you spoken to those people yet?"

"We believe the weapon used to kill her was some kind of sniper rifle," DI Smyth said. "And as such the killer could have been quite some distance away."

"Are you saying it's the same killer as the other ones in the papers?"

"We believe so. But we also believe these murders were not simply the work of a madman who selects his victims at random. Something has to link these people. Do the names Charles Lincoln and Diana Wells mean anything to you?"

"I've never heard of them."

"Are you positive about that?"

"Absolutely. I've never heard those names before."

DI Smyth stood up and gestured to Yang Chu to do the same.

"We are very sorry for your loss, Mr Price. We will definitely need to speak to you again, but in the meantime, if you think of anything that might be relevant to your wife's killing, please call me."

He handed Price one of his cards.

"What do you think?" Yang Chu asked DI Smyth as they drove away from the industrial estate.

"He had nothing to do with it."

"How can you be so sure?"

"His body language suggested to me he was telling the truth. Besides he was in London until this morning. We'll look at his alibi, but I get the impression it'll check out."

"He could have arranged for someone else to shoot his wife. He's obviously not short of a few bob and you know what the Russians are like."

"Attaching stereotypes does not solve murder investigations, detective. You mark my words, what happened to Wendy Price had nothing to do with her husband."

"You said you spent ten years in the army?" Yang Chu said. "What was it like? I mean what was it like in Iraq and Afghanistan?"

"I was in Intelligence," DI Smyth replied. "I didn't see any action – I was more of a tactical adviser."

"And what made you join the police? Was it because of your uncle?"

"Uncle Jeremy had nothing to do with my decision. In fact, if I see him once every few years it's a lot. He and my father don't exactly see eye to eye and that's all I'm going to say on the matter. I came to York because it has an exceptional clear-up record."

"Most of that has been down to Smith," Yang Chu told him.

"The legendary DS Smith. There are few policemen who haven't heard of DS Smith. I believe he was overlooked for the DI position. Do you know why that was? Surely, with his record he would have been the obvious choice?"

"It's a long story," Yang Chu didn't feel like elaborating. "Let's just say he had a bit of an altercation with your uncle."

"Interesting. And from now on I would appreciate it if you would refer to him as Superintendent Smyth. As I intend to."

Yang Chu had just turned off the engine when DI Smyth's mobile phone started to ring. He took it out and pressed, *answer*.

Yang Chu watched as DI Smyth listened to whoever was on the other end. His facial expression remained the same throughout.

"Thank you, Mr Price," he said and ended the call.

He turned to Yang Chu. "Mr Price remembered something about his wife."

"Go on."

"When Wendy Price met Dmitri she was already married to another man. She filed for divorce and married Dmitri as soon as it was finalised. Her ex-husband took it rather badly according to Price."

"Do you think he's responsible for killing her?" Yang Chu said. "That seems a bit far-fetched if you ask me. It's one thing to be bitter about losing your wife to another man, but it's another thing altogether to kill her because of it."

"There's more. Wendy's ex was serving a term in Afghanistan when Wendy wrote to him about the divorce, and the most intriguing part is what he did in the army. Wendy's ex-husband was an experienced sniper."

CHAPTER TWENTY FOUR

Smith woke and for a second he'd forgotten where he was. The pain in his head was almost gone. The throbbing pain he'd felt earlier had been replaced with a dull ache over his eye. He had a tube in his arm that was feeding small quantities of paracetamol at regular intervals into his bloodstream. He sat up in bed and picked up his mobile phone. It was almost noon. He looked around the room and realised that all hospital wards looked exactly the same. They all had the same bed sheets, the same sterile tiles on the floor and they all smelled the same. The doctor who had been treating him came in the room.
"How are you feeling?"
"Back to normal," Smith said. "I really don't think it's necessary to keep me in overnight. Somebody else might need this bed."
Smith had always hated hospitals. Considering how much time he'd spent in them, he never seemed to get used to them.
"It's entirely up to you," Dr Barnes told him. "You are not a prisoner here, but I would advise you to let us keep an eye on you at least until tomorrow morning."
Smith thought hard. He knew that Whitton would not be too happy if he discharged himself from hospital again and for that reason alone, he decided to listen to the doctor's advice for once.
"I'll do what you say. Can I ask you something though?"
"Of course."
"You told me earlier that these migraine attacks often come on after periods of extreme stress?"
"That's correct," Dr Barnes said. "Have you been under stress recently?"
Smith laughed. "Sorry, but my job seems to attract stress. There was this case we were working on earlier in the year. Some madman had assumed

the role of God and was killing people for their sins. Anyway, during that investigation I did something really stupid. This isn't going to go any further is it?"

"Of course not."

"I had too much to drink one night and I ended up in bed with one of my colleagues. This madman somehow found out about this and I was very nearly the final victim. I was almost killed."

"That does sound incredibly stressful."

"That's not all. I couldn't bear it anymore – it was eating away at my insides, so I had to tell my wife what had happened."

"I see," was all Dr Barnes said.

"She took it very badly," Smith couldn't understand why he was finding it so easy to talk to a stranger about this. "She moved out and took our four-year-old daughter with her. That was two months ago."

"She was obviously very concerned about you when you were brought in this morning."

"That's just the thing – things seem to be getting better between us. We've stopped bickering and I've made it very clear that I'm prepared to wait as long as it takes for her to be ready. It's been a rough couple of months but I feel more relaxed about everything than I've felt in a very long time."

"Such is the nature of migraines," Dr Barnes said. "They often attack when you least expect it. When the stress subsides for example. The research in this field is still very much in its infancy but there have been studies that show how stress can trigger a certain reaction in the neurons that transmit signals to the brain. When that stress is over these neurons contract and this is what can trigger an attack. I'm afraid I need to go and check on some patients."

"No worries," Smith said. "Thank you so much for listening."

He left the room and Smith was left to try and process what he'd just been told. The more he thought about it the more it made sense. For as long as he could remember, he had always been under more pressure than anyone should have to bear. The very nature of his job and his determination to bring every case to its rightful conclusion demanded it. More recently there had been a period of calm in his life – not much had happened at work and he and Whitton were moving closer to some kind of reconciliation.

I can't win, he thought.

From what the doctor had told him, in order to prevent a migraine attack he either needed to remain permanently under stress or avoid any kind of stress altogether and he knew for certain that the latter was simply not an option.

His phone beeped to let him know he'd received a message. He opened it up and saw it was from Whitton. He had a smile on his face until he read the words on the screen.

Young man shot dead close to the Minster.
It looks like we've got another one.

CHAPTER TWENTY FIVE

Whitton and Bridge stood with Grant Webber inside the police tape that had been put up to prevent anyone getting near the body. The dead man was lying on his side with his eyes wide open. What was once the top of his head was now gone. A white baseball cap lay on the ground a few metres behind him. It was stained deep crimson and thick globules of bloody skin and grey brain matter were spattered all around it. Some of the blood on the cap was still wet and it glistened in the midday sun.

"What the hell is happening in this town?" Grant Webber said. "This is the fourth one in as many days."

"It looks like we've got a real whacko on the loose," Bridge said.

"Very eloquently put," Webber said. "But I must admit I'm inclined to agree with you."

"And if it is the same killer, he's also a serial killer, isn't he?" Bridge added.

"Do we know who the dead man is?" Whitton asked.

"He had some ID in a wallet in his jacket pocket," Webber said. "But unless he looks extremely good for his sixty-eight years and he's changed his appearance drastically so he no longer looks like the photograph of Haki Nakamono that was on the photo on the driving licence, I'd hazard a guess that he's one of York's less upstanding citizens. Other than the wallet I didn't find anything else on him."

DI Oliver Smyth arrived with DC Yang Chu.

"We came as soon as we heard," Smyth said. "What have we got?"

Webber told him.

"Another one then?" DI Smyth said when the Head of Forensics had finished. "I think we can assume so. We don't have any ID yet."

"I know him," Yang Chu had taken a closer look. "Even with the top of his head missing, I'd recognise those shifty eyes anywhere. It's Liam Lovelake. We've pulled him a few times for petty stuff. Robbing tourists mostly."

"He had the wallet of a Japanese man in his jacket pocket," Webber told him.

"That sounds like Lovelake."

"Well at least this time the shooter has done us a favour," Bridge chipped in. "There's one less scrote on the streets."

"I'll have no talk like that from anyone on my team," DI Smyth moved so close to Bridge that Bridge thought he was about to be physically attacked.

"Sorry, sir," he said. "I have a habit of thinking out loud sometimes."

"We've got an interesting lead on the woman who was shot outside the supermarket," Yang Chu said. "Mrs Price's husband told us something about her ex. Robert King. Apparently, he took the break-up very badly."

"That's still no reason to kill her," Whitton said. "And why would he kill all the others? It doesn't make sense."

"We haven't figured that out yet, but this is the interesting part: The bloke's ex-army. He served in Afghanistan a few years back as a sniper. The man happens to be an extremely experienced marksman."

"Bloody hell," Bridge exclaimed. "Then it has to be him. Have you spoken to him yet?"

"That's been a bit of a problem," DI Smyth said. "We can't seem to find the man – he called in sick at work almost a week ago and he hasn't been seen at home in that same period of time."

"It has to be him," Bridge said again.

"Let's not jump to conclusions before we've spoken to him," DI Smyth said.

"With respect, sir, the bloke suddenly disappears into thin air the same time somebody decides to start taking pot-shots at people. Surely that has to be more than a coincidence."

"I'm not doubting your reasoning, Bridge," DI Smyth said. "And I for one believe there is no such thing as coincidence."

Whitton smiled.

Someone I know is going to get on just fine with you, she thought.

"We've put out his description," DI Smyth continued. "And we've got people in touch with the airports and ferry terminals. If he's left the country, we'll soon know about it. For all we know he's simply jetted off on a sneaky summer holiday."

"You don't sound too convinced, sir," Whitton said.

"No, I'm not. Right now, he's all we've got and we're going to concentrate all our efforts on finding this Robert King. As I said, we've put his description out there but in the meantime what I want to do is search his house. And for that I'll need reasonable grounds, so let's see if we can find some. I want that house searched whether he's at home or not."

Bridge frowned. He took an A4-sized sheet of paper from his pocket and unfolded it. "What did you say the bloke's name was again?"

"Robert King," DI Smyth replied.

Bridge showed him the sheet of paper. "This is a printout we got from the Chairman of the Greyham Rifle and Pistol Club. He gave us names and contact details of all the top marksmen at the club. Robert King's name is at the very top."

CHAPTER TWENTY SIX

Helmand Province, Southern Afghanistan
A few years earlier

"Welly," Private King shouted. "Your scope is fucking filthy. When was the last time you cleaned it?"
"I'm not your skivvy," the man nicknamed *Welly* replied.
"No, you're supposed to be my spotter. Now do your job. You're half-blind as it is – you'll be even more useless with a dirty scope."
Welly muttered something under his breath but headed for the toilets to do as he'd been asked.
"What's that idiot even doing here?" Private Peter Meek said.
Meek was practising alongside King at the range in Camp Bastion. A competition was about to start, and they had half an hour left to set their scopes and gauge the wind.
"I don't actually know to be honest," King said. "He just seems to mill around the barracks most of the time."
   Welly returned with the scope. "I've cleaned it as best as I could."
"I should think so," King said. "Train it on the seven-hundred far to the right. I need to get this scope right if I'm going to retain my title."
Welly lay flat on the ground next to King. He focussed the scope until the outer circle was in line with the outer on the target.
"Got it," he said.
"Now, shut the hell up," King ordered. "This is important."
He prepared for the shot the same way he always did. With his eyes closed he breathed in deeply and counted to ten. Then he opened his eyes and looked through the telescopic sight. The wind was light today and the 700

shouldn't prove to be much of a challenge. He'd made the shot a hundred times before.

"I'm going for the test," he told Welly. "Let me know if I need to adjust."

He pressed the trigger gently, there was a crack and King remained still.

"Miss," Welly told him.

King turned to look at his spotter. "What do you mean, *miss*? From what I was looking at I was dead in the centre. Were you even looking at the right target?"

"Of course I was – 700, furthest to the left."

"Right you arsehole," King raised his voice. "Furthest to the right. Are you fucking stupid as well as blind?"

"Sorry, I thought you said left."

"Idiot. Let's get it right this time, shall we? Far right."

He repeated the process and fired another shot.

"Ten, just off the centre." Welly informed him.

"That's better."

King fired off another six shots and sat up. "That'll do me. What's the damage?"

"Five tens," Welly said. "And one nine, just outside the line. Can I make a couple of shots?"

King looked at his spotter as though he'd asked him for a kiss. "Are you taking the piss?"

"You've still got two cartridges left. I just want to have a go."

"You do not *have a go* with an Arctic L96," King scoffed.

Out of spite he got down into position once more and fired off the remaining two cartridges, aiming at nothing in particular.

"We've got ten minutes before the comp starts, so I suggest you relieve that pea-bladder of yours, so you don't need to go while we're competing."

Welly got up and headed back to the toilets.

*　*　*

The shooting competition had reached the halfway stage. Private King was level on points with an old rival from another regiment. Private Robert Oxley had definitely improved since their last meeting – even King had to admit that, and it was going to be close shooting in the second half.
Oxley was due to shoot first. King watched him closely and swore under his breath when he heard Oxley's spotter.
"Ten. Dead centre."
The adjudicator confirmed it and it was time for King to shoot.
He controlled his breathing and matched his rival's shot.
Oxley, ten – King, Ten.

And so it carried on through to the final round. They each had one shot left. If Oxley shot a ten here, King would need at least maximum points just to enter the sudden-death stage.
Oxley hit a dead-centre ten.
King steadied himself and aimed. The inner circle was now a mess – they would need to replace the targets if the competition went into sudden-death. The wind was picking up from the side, but King hadn't noticed it. Often it was the spotter who picked up on subtle changes in wind speed and direction, but Welly hadn't appeared to notice it either. King concentrated hard on the centre of the target and pressed the trigger.
"Shit," he heard Welly say. "Eight. Right over."
King's head slumped forwards. He had finally been beaten by Private Robert Oxley. He got to his feet and as he did so he felt the brisk breeze on his face.
He turned to look at Welly, who had also stood up. "When did the wind pick up?"
"I didn't notice it until you were about to make the final shot."

"And you didn't think it might be a good idea to inform me?" King could feel his heartbeat increasing.

"I didn't think it would make much difference."

"I…" King started to speak.

He glared at Welly and stormed off in the direction of the barracks, leaving his rifle on the ground behind him.

* * *

Hours later, the lights had gone out and the barracks were silent apart from the odd cough or snore. Welly lay awake in his bed with his eyes open. He couldn't sleep. The look Private King had given him after the shooting competition had unnerved him. He was well aware of King's quick temper, and worse still he knew King had a mean streak a mile long. King was a man who was used to getting his own way and when that didn't happen he was capable of almost anything.

Welly's eyes were now feeling heavy and he felt them close of their own accord. He drifted off for a few seconds then opened his eyes suddenly. He'd heard a noise that didn't sound right. It wasn't the familiar sound of men sleeping, it was something else – a shuffling sound like feet with socks on creeping across tiles. The sound disappeared, but Welly lay awake waiting. He didn't hear the sound again and he slowly drifted back to sleep.

He was woken sometime later by an agonising pain inside his left leg. It felt like concentrated acid was burning a hole in it. The pain increased in intensity until Welly could take it no more. He shot up in bed and screamed. His whole inside leg was now on fire and he was having difficulty breathing. Even though it was chilly in the barracks Welly was starting to sweat. He tried to get to his feet, but his left leg wouldn't obey and he fell to the ground.

A few of the lighter sleepers had heard the commotion and lights were being turned on. Corporal George Peters was first out of bed.

"What the hell is going on?"

"My leg is in agony," Welly rasped. "And I can hardly breathe."

Peters carefully removed the blankets from Welly's bed and gasped. There at the end of the bed was a fully-grown yellow scorpion. Welly's vision was now blurred but he could still make out Private Rob King in the bunk a few bunks down from his. King was sitting up in bed and Welly was sure he had a grin on his face.

CHAPTER TWENTY SEVEN

"We've got a lot to go over," DI Smyth said in the conference room. "So, let's make a start. We're a bit short-staffed at the moment what with Smith's incident this morning, but we'll carry on regardless. How is Smith by the way?"

He addressed this question to Whitton.

"They're keeping him in overnight," she told him. "But there's no reason why he shouldn't be discharged and back at work tomorrow."

"Good. I want to try something that proved to be very successful in Manchester."

He approached the whiteboard and started to write. First, he wrote the names of each victim at the top, beginning with Charles Lincoln and finally, Liam Lovelake on the right-hand side."

"These shootings all happened within a very short space of time," he said. "Lincoln was shot around eight-thirty on Friday morning – Diana Wells at nine-thirty in the evening on the same day, Wendy Price yesterday at five in the afternoon and finally, Liam Lovelake who was gunned down earlier today. What does that tell us?"

"The shooter doesn't have a job, or he's on leave." Bridge was the first to speak.

"Good," DI Smyth said. "And could we please refrain from using that term. I hate it to be honest. Anything else?"

"He's in a hurry?" Yang Chu suggested.

"Interesting point. What else?"

Silence.

"Throw something at me," DI Smyth urged. "Think out loud. It's often when you let yourselves go that the answer comes right out."

"Following on from Yang Chu's suggestion." It was Whitton. "Why is he in a hurry? Surely his MO offers him as much time as he wants."

"Maybe he's enjoying it," Yang Chu said. "He could have spent weeks if not months setting everything up and now he's enjoying the fruits of his labours."

"Or he could be out of control," Baldwin spoke for the first time.

"I don't think so," Whitton argued. "Everything we've seen so far indicates a cool, calculated killer. The planning has been meticulous, and the final kill is carried out with precision. I don't think this killer is out of control."

"It was just a suggestion," Baldwin did not look happy.

"And that's what we want," DI Smyth said. "Empty your heads of every possible scenario and the correct one is sure to come along sooner or later."

Grant Webber came in with Gwen Culvert. Bridge was certain she was even shorter today. She was carrying a folder that was almost as big as she was.

"Sorry we're late," the Head of Forensics apologised for them both. "But we have something concrete at long last. We're yet to analyse the cartridge that killed Liam Lovelake earlier today, but we can confirm that all three of the others were shot from the same gun, so we now know we're looking at the same gunman."

"That's something at least," DI Smyth said.

"And," Webber wasn't finished yet. "Gwen is finished with the ballistics reports for the first three shootings. Gwen."

"Thank you, Grant," the diminutive ballistics expert said. "Charles Lincoln was shot from a distance of six hundred metres."

She opened up the folder and passed some files around.

"These are the topographic and 3D elevation reports. If you will be so kind as to have a look. Where those two red lines cross is an estimation of the location of where the shot was taken from."

"How accurate is this?" Bridge asked.

"To the nearest five metres."

"That's quite impressive."

"This is close to where I live," Yang Chu exclaimed. "If I'm not mistaken there's a bunch of student houses around the area you've marked on the map."

By the time they'd analysed all three ballistics reports the team were quite certain of one thing – the gunman had used a different location each time.

"Why does he change locations?" Bridge asked.

"I think he's lessening the chances of us finding him," Whitton said. "If he shot these people from the same place each time, the better the chance we'd have of finding something."

"So, we can assume he's not making the shot from his own place?" Yang Chu said.

"Agreed," DI Smyth said. "But how is he gaining access to these locations?"

"A lot of student houses are standing empty at this time of year," Yang Chu pointed out. "The semester has just finished and most of the students will have gone home or abroad."

"Do you think he's breaking into these places?" Baldwin said.

"Possibly," DI Smyth said. "We know he's capable of cold-blooded murder, so a simple break-in isn't going to rattle him."

"There's something bothering me about the shooting of Wendy Price," Whitton said.

"Let's hear it," DI Smyth urged.

"It's the trajectory," Whitton continued. "It's not right."

"Are you saying I made a mistake?" Gwen Culvert said.

"Of course not. I mean it's not right in that it's too low. The first two shootings were carried out from above the victim, but unless I'm mistaken,

Mrs Price was shot from below. How can that be possible? I know the supermarket where she died. It's pretty flat around there and the terrain remains flat for quite some distance around it."

"What's this place here?" DI Smyth pointed to a spot on the map.

"That's an old industrial estate," Yang Chu said. "You don't want to know what goes on around there at night."

"The shooter was in a car when he made the shot," Bridge said and instantly regretted it. "Sorry, I mean the gunman."

"I think Bridge is right," Grant Webber said. "The height where Gwen has deduced the shot was taken from is around the height of the window of an average car."

"And the gunman would have had a clear shot of the supermarket car park if he was parked by the old warehouses," Yang Chu added.

"Right," DI Smyth said. "Unfortunately, it is not going to be an early finish for any of us today. I'm not up to speed with regards to my predecessor's view on coffee breaks, but I for one could kill for a strong coffee right now, and I'm ordering you all to take a break and recharge your batteries. We'll reconvene in thirty minutes. I think you'll all agree that this has been a most productive briefing."

CHAPTER TWENTY EIGHT

"What do you make of the new DI?" Bridge asked in the canteen. Whitton, Yang Chu and Bridge were sat by the window in the canteen. PC Baldwin had declined the offer to join them and Grant Webber had something to discuss with DCI Chalmers.

"He's nothing like how I pictured him," Yang Chu said.

"Me neither," Bridge agreed. "I expected a lower-ranked version of the Super, but he's nothing like old Smyth."

"I actually think Smith is finally going to have a boss who thinks along the same lines as him," Whitton said. "Some of the things DI Smyth came out with were uncannily like the stuff my husband says."

"Like the *I don't believe in coincidence* thing?" Yang Chu said.

"Exactly."

"He'll be banging on about motive next," Bridge added.

"Well I've been pleasantly surprised so far," Whitton said.

"We were chatting on the way back from talking to Wendy Price's husband," Yang Chu said. "And I get the impression that he doesn't really get on with his uncle."

"Isn't that how he got the job in the first place?" Bridge asked.

"Apparently not," Whitton said. "And you can see how sharp he is – he doesn't need old Smyth's help."

"I like the way he lets us say what we're thinking," Yang Chu said. "There were a few ridiculous suggestions made back there and he didn't knock any of them. I suppose we'd better get back in there.

"I hope the break had the desired effect," DI Smyth said back in the conference room. "This is how we're going to play it. Tomorrow, I want you to find out as much as you can about each of the victims. I imagine you're wondering why I didn't make that a priority straight away."

"It did cross my mind," Bridge admitted.

"And so it should have. In my experience, speaking to those closest to murder victims immediately after their deaths has, in most cases been a complete waste of time. The family and friends are distraught, and in shock and as such their minds are not working like they usually are. After even a short period of time they are thinking much more clearly and that is when we'll find out more about the victims. Right now, I want to concentrate on one man – Robert King. King is the ex-husband of the third victim, Wendy Price. Not only did King take the fact of his wife marrying another man extremely badly, he also happens to be an ex-army sniper. Unfortunately, Mr King appears to have disappeared into thin air, but we are making every effort to apprehend him. Given that the last time the man was seen corresponds with the time these shootings started, Robert King is our number one suspect at the moment. Any questions?"

"Are we going to search his house?" Bridge asked. "You said something about getting authorisation to search his house."

DI Smyth sighed. "Yes, I did, but to obtain a search warrant we need a certain amount of justification."

"Surely the fact that he was unhappy about his wife running away with another bloke and that he's a hotshot deadeye will count for something."

"I don't think it will, so I'm going to be brutally honest with you. I'm going to go down a route I wouldn't normally go down – I'm going to play the nepotism card."

Nobody spoke for a few moments.

"You're going to use your family connection with the Super?" Whitton was the first one brave enough to say what everybody else was thinking.

"Exactly. I will convince Superintendent Smyth that it is imperative we obtain a search warrant."

"I can't see anything wrong with that," Bridge said. "It's the truth."

"Good. Let's move on, shall we."

Three and a half hours later the whole team was exhausted. DI Smyth had decided to everyone's relief that they were not going to get any further today. They had a clear plan of action for the next day – they needed to speak with the relatives and friends of the victims as well as the people on the list Bridge had received from the Chairman of the Greyham Rifle and Pistol Club. DI Smyth was going to speak to his uncle about procuring a warrant to search Robert King's house. Smyth brought the briefing to a close and told them to all be back at seven the next morning.

"I'm totally done in," Bridge said. "I'm going to knock back a few pints then it's straight off to bed. Anyone feel like joining me? For the knocking back a few pints part, I mean."

"I've got a hungry little girl to look after," Whitton reminded him.

"Your parents can look after Laura. Come on – when was the last time we went out for a few drinks after work?"

"I promised Smith I'd go and visit him at the hospital."

"He's being released tomorrow," Bridge insisted. "He won't mind if you don't go and see him later. Come on, I'm buying."

"One drink," Whitton gave in. "I'll have to phone my mum and dad and ask them if it's alright to look after Laura first."

"What about you?" Bridge asked Yang Chu.

"I reckon I'll be asleep after one pint. Maybe some other time."

"Lightweight."

* * *

Whitton and Bridge walked inside the Hog's Head. It was Monday and Whitton was surprised at how many of the tables were occupied. Marge, the owner was pulling a pint of bitter behind the bar.

"Hi, Marge," Whitton said. "How are you?"

"I've been a bit ill, love," Marge replied. "A touch of the flu, but it's just about cleared up. It's lovely to see you again. Where's that husband of yours?"

She frowned at Bridge.

"He's in hospital again," Whitton didn't feel like explaining that they had separated.

"Hospital? Nothing serious I hope?"

"He had a severe migraine attack, but the doctor said he'll be fine. They're keeping him in overnight to be on the safe side."

"He works too hard," Marge said. "Migraines can be caused by stress – Jason needs to slow down a bit."

"Do you want to tell him that?"

Marge smiled. "What can I get you? Are you going to have a bite to eat?"

"Just a couple of pints please. Theakstons and a pint of lager for DS Bridge here."

"Coming right up."

They took their drinks to one of the empty tables and sat down.

"Cheers," Bridge raised his glass in the air.

"What are we drinking to?" Whitton asked.

"I don't know. To the new DI. A Smyth with an IQ in double figures."

"You're terrible. Did you see how his whole demeanour changed when he spoke about asking the Super to help with a search warrant?"

"I know – I wonder what that's all about."

"Maybe it's some kind of family feud."

"Anyway, this Rob King bloke is our shooter, you'll see."

"Why do you keep calling him that?" Whitton took a sip of her beer.

"It sounds all Hollywood," Bridge smiled. "It makes the job seem more exciting, don't you think. Are you and Smith getting back together?"

"Why do people keep asking me that?"

"Because you and Smith are made for each other. You were born to be together. And if you don't forgive him, he's going to spend the rest of his life a lonely, miserable old man."

"That's a bit melodramatic. Do you really think this Rob King is the gunman?"

"It all makes sense. He's an expert deadeye, and he's also pissed off because his wife ran off with another man. It's him."

"I suppose we'll know more tomorrow when we've spoken to the other members of the gun club, and speaking of tomorrow, I'm off."

"You've been here five minutes," Bridge said. "And you haven't even finished your pint."

Whitton picked up her glass and drained its contents in five seconds flat.

"There, are you happy now. I'll see you bright and early in the morning."

CHAPTER TWENTY NINE

"I need to get to work," Smith told the nurse who had come to check on him. "I need to go home and change and then I need to get to work. Who do I speak to about getting me out of here?"
The nurse shook his head. "You do seem to be much better this morning. How's the head?"
"One hundred percent," Smith lied.
There was still a dull throbbing over his left eye, but he decided he'd had worse.
"Could you please find someone to come and let me out?"
  Ten minutes later, Dr Barnes came inside the room and stopped by the bed. Smith was already fully dressed and sitting on the edge of the bed.
"How are you feeling?" Dr Barnes asked.
"I'll be better when I get out of here," Smith told him. "There's nothing wrong with me.
Dr Barnes nodded. "You do have some colour in your face this morning. I'd like you to take this and hand it in to the pharmacy. I've also taken the liberty of signing a document that states you are fit to return to work. I know how petty they can be in your profession."
He handed Smith a prescription and a doctor's note.
"Thanks," Smith said. "I appreciate it. What's the prescription for?"
"It's similar to Ibuprofen, but only available with a prescription. Try to keep some at hand wherever you go, and whenever you notice the warning signs take two tablets as soon as possible."
"Warning signs?"
"If you feel a tension above one eye," Dr Barnes elaborated. "Or you feel the onset of the aura, take the medication and most of the time the full migraine will not materialise."

"And if it does?"

"We'll deal with that when it happens. Good luck, DS Smith."

Theakston and Fred were more annoyed than happy to see Smith. The old Bull Terrier and the repulsive Pug were clearly not pleased about being left outside all night. Smith let them in through the back door and filled both their bowls to the brim with food. It was only after they'd eaten every last morsel that they even acknowledged Smith.

"I'm sorry, boys," Smith leaned down and patted them both. "This time it wasn't my fault. I'm afraid I'm going to have to love you and leave you again. I'll make it up to you, I promise."

He opened the back door again and both dogs looked at him as though he'd lost his mind. Fred seemed especially displeased. The Pug's eyes bulged out as he glared at Smith.

"Do I have to remind you that you are actually dogs?" Smith said as they both stubbornly refused to go back outside. "And that normally means that I'm *your* boss and not the other way around."

Eventually they conceded, but not without scowling at Smith to let him know how annoyed they were with him.

After a quick shower and a change of clothes Smith made his way to work. He realised he'd left the bag containing the prescription he'd picked up from the pharmacy on the kitchen table while he was enduring the wrath of the dogs. He didn't feel like going back and getting it and he reckoned another migraine attack so soon after the first one was highly unlikely. The weather was definitely changing. The clear skies of the past few days were gone. Ominous grey shapes were forming in the sky and Smith had been in Yorkshire long enough to know that rain wasn't far away. He parked his car next to Yang Chu's Ford Focus and went inside the station. Yet another unfamiliar face sat behind the front desk. Smith made his way to his office and as he opened the door he heard the sound of raised voices coming from further down the corridor. They appeared to be coming from the direction of Superintendent Smyth's office. Smith walked towards them and stopped a short distance away. The door was closed. Smith stood and listened. He couldn't make out every word but whoever was inside with the Superintendent was talking very loudly about something. The words, *Greece* and *Golf* came up on more than one occasion. The voices stopped and Smith turned around and headed back to his office. He was just about to go inside when DI Smyth walked past him without saying a word. He looked extremely angry. Smith turned on his computer and quickly checked his emails. There was nothing that needed his attention urgently, so he turned off the PC and left the office.

He bumped into Whitton in the corridor.
"How are you feeling?"
"You're the third person who's asked me that this morning," Smith told her.
"I feel loved. What's happening?"
"We're all waiting for the DI," Whitton said. "It's a long story but he reluctantly agreed to persuade his uncle to speed up a search warrant for Robert King's place. I get the feeling they don't exactly see eye to eye."
"I can see that. I just overheard a pretty heated conversation, and the DI didn't exactly seem pleased afterwards."
"Well, I just hope he managed to organise the warrant."

She filled Smith in on the plan of action for the day. The DI had called a short briefing and then they were to speak to relatives and friends of the victims as well as the most experienced marksmen from the local gun club. Smith and Whitton walked inside the small conference room together. Bridge and Yang Chu were already seated as was PC Baldwin. Grant Webber was sitting next to Gwen Culvert. Dr Kenny Bean, the Head of Pathology was also there. DI Smyth was nowhere to be seen.

"Morning, Kenny," Smith sat next to the portly pathologist. "What brings you here?"

"All in good time, my friend," Dr Bean said. "All in good time."

"Why do you always have to be so cryptic?"

"I don't like repeating myself," Dr Bean said. "So I'll wait for Oliver to arrive if it's alright by you."

DI Smyth came in ten minutes later. He was very red in the face.
"Sorry for the delay, but I had some urgent matters to sort out. We'll briefly go over what we discussed in the briefing yesterday, and then Dr Bean can fill us in on what Pathology has come up with. Grant, do you have anything else to add?"

"We've gone over all the likely spots where the gunman made his shots," Webber said. "And we found nothing to indicate a rifle was fired at any of them. No spent cartridges, nothing. Either the gunman didn't shoot from there or he was very careful, and he took everything away with him."

"He's been very meticulous so far," Smith said. "So, I don't think he would leave anything behind at the scenes."

"I'm still waiting to hear on the progress of the search warrant," DI Smyth said. "So, until we have confirmation, I want Smith and Whitton to speak to Gordon Wells. Hopefully he will be in more of a state to talk to us now. Bridge, you and Baldwin can see if you can find out anything more from Dmitri Price. He's the one who gave us Robert King, so maybe there's more he can tell us about his wife's ex. I don't believe we're going to get anything more out of Charles Lincoln's partner so Yang Chu, you're coming with me to dig around in the life of Liam Lovelake."

"You'd better wear protective clothing," Bridge said. "Lovelake tended to associate with only the bottom-feeders of society."

"Kenny," Smyth turned to the Head of Pathology. "The floor's yours."

"Thank you, Oliver," Dr Bean said. "We're not finished with the young man who was gunned down yesterday, but I thought you'd like an update on the first three. Cause of death for all three was definitely due to the severe trauma caused by the high calibre bullet. It's as simple as that. TOD for Charles Lincoln was just after eight in the morning on Friday, but there were so many witnesses that we knew that already. Diana Wells died between eight and ten that same evening and Wendy Price's heart stopped beating just after 5pm on Sunday. We also have witnesses there. Right, what I am here to tell you today is we found something interesting with the second victim, Diana Wells. She too died due to the damage from the bullet, but it appears Mrs Wells was not the only one killed by that bullet – she was roughly three months pregnant."

CHAPTER THIRTY

"That poor man," Whitton said.

She and Smith were on their way towards the new development where Diana Wells was shot. They'd arranged to speak to her husband, Gordon. He'd been reluctant at first, but Smith had managed to persuade him how important it was and he'd agreed to give them a few minutes of his time.

"To lose your wife and baby like that must be awful," Whitton added.

"That's probably why he was so distraught," Smith remembered.

Gordon Wells had been inconsolable. He'd been in no state to talk to anybody.

"That's two murders," Whitton said. "A mother and an unborn child. Whoever did this needs to be put away forever."

"You know as well as I do an unborn child has no rights. This is one murder according to the law."

"Well, I think the law needs changing. Wow, look at this place."

"Gordon Wells has the penthouse," Smith told her.

They made their way up in the lift and emerged onto the impressive landing. Smith had been inside the Wells' penthouse before, so he headed straight for it. Gordon Wells opened the door before Smith had even pressed the buzzer. He didn't look well at all. His face was grey and puffy and heavy blue bags hung under his eyes. The last time Smith had seen him he'd been lying in the foetal position on the floor, groaning like a wounded animal, so this was at least a slight improvement.

"Mr Wells," Smith said. "This is DC Whitton."

"You'd better come in," Gordon opened the door wider.

Smith and Whitton went inside. The first thing Smith noticed was the window that the bullet had penetrated had been replaced.

"I couldn't bear looking at it," Gordon had seen him looking at the huge window. "Would you like something to drink?"

"No thank you," Smith said. "I'm sorry about this but we didn't get a chance to talk to you the other day."

"I didn't know what was happening," Gordon sat down on an armchair. "It was like being in a dream where it's impossible to wake up."

"I know this is hard, Mr Wells," Smith said. "But can you tell us what happened when you got home last Friday?"

"I got home just after eleven," Gordon began.

"Where had you been?" Whitton asked him.

"I was working late at the office."

"Until eleven at night?" Smith said.

"My job is not nine-to-five. I run an IT company that specialises in automation."

"I'm not much of a computer expert," Smith admitted. "What's automation?"

"Let's say you're away on holiday," Gordon said. "And you want your property to appear lived in. I install systems that can switch on your lights, close curtains, turn on the television etc. Anybody watching the property would assume there is somebody in the house. And when you return home, you can turn on the central heating, or air con. And all this can be done via an app on your mobile phone. I've also moved into automated security systems. No offence but with the rising crime in this city, it's a booming business. I've got packages that allow you to monitor your home from your mobile phone."

"That's amazing," Smith said. "Can you design a system that can feed two grumpy dogs when I'm not home?"

"That would be easy."

"OK," Whitton said. "So, you came home just after eleven and found your wife. What did you do then?"

"I can't actually remember," Gordon replied. "It's all a bit of a blur. But my neighbour in one of the other penthouses told me he was woken up by me banging on the door. He led me inside and went to see what the problem was and then he phoned the police. He's an ex Chief Constable, you know."

"I have to ask you this, Mr Wells," Smith said. "Is there anyone who can confirm you were at work that night?"

"No," Gordon said quite matter-of-factly. "I was alone in the office."

"I see. So, there is nobody to corroborate this?"

"Nobody," Gordon said. "As in no human being, but there will be electronic proof. My whereabouts that night will be logged in the system."

"What do you mean?" Smith was confused.

"Whatever you do on our system leaves some kind of trail," Gordon explained. "I am the only one in the company who has access to the central system inside the office and you are more than welcome to send one of your experts in to check."

"We will," Smith said. "Can you think of anybody who could possibly want to kill your wife?"

"Of course not. Diana had no enemies. She was a quiet soul. Of course, sometimes when she was in her writing zone, she could become quite antisocial, but she was an artist and it goes with the territory."

Smith had been thinking hard how to bring up the next topic of conversation. Gordon Wells appeared to be reasonably calm, so he decided to just come straight to the point.

"Mr Wells, were you aware that your wife was pregnant?"

Gordon's calm demeanour changed in an instant. His eyes darkened, he glared at Smith and then seemed to focus on something on the floor.

"Of course I was aware. What the hell are you trying to imply here?"

"I'm sorry," Smith said. "I'm not implying anything."

"Diana and I had been trying for quite some time," Gordon's eyes had now filled with tears. "At one stage we didn't know if we would even be able to have children, then Diana came home and told me the news. I was the happiest man in the world. And now this…"

He stopped there, stood up and walked over to the window. "All this means nothing really, does it?"

Smith and Whitton didn't know what to say.

"This view," Gordon continued. "This expensive view. All the money in the world means absolutely nothing when something like this happens."

He turned around. Tears were streaming down his face.

"You will catch whoever did this, won't you?"

"Yes," Smith replied without thinking. "We're going to catch whoever did this."

CHAPTER THIRTY ONE

"DI Smyth has organised the search warrant," Bridge told Smith on Whitton's phone outside the apartment block where Gordon Wells lived. "He wants you there when they go in."

"Why didn't he phone me directly?" Smith asked.

"Apparently he did, but you didn't answer,"

Smith checked his pockets. His mobile phone wasn't there. Then he remembered he'd put it down on the kitchen table with the prescription and had forgotten to pick it up again before he left the house.

"What about Whitton?"

"I'm on my way to speak to one of the top shooter's," Bridge told him. "You can drop her off there and me and Whitton can speak to him together."

He gave Smith the address as well as the address for Robert King.

"DI Smyth wants me there when they search Robert King's place," Smith handed the phone back to Whitton. "He said the DI asked for me specifically."

"You're going to enjoy working with him," Whitton said.

"What makes you say that?"

"I just get this feeling – you two are so alike it's uncanny."

"I don't know how to react to that."

"Take it as a compliment. What did you make of Gordon Wells?"

"I'm not quite sure," Smith admitted. "The last time I saw him he was curled up on the floor wailing like a baby, but today he seemed somehow detached from everything that's happened."

"Shock is a funny thing. I still feel sorry for the poor bloke. Losing your wife and child in one go must be the worst thing in the world."

"We still need to get one of the IT guys to check his alibi."

"Of course, but I can't see how he's involved in any way. He seems to be the one who earns the money."

"You should know by now that it's not always about money."

"Listen to us," Whitton smiled. "This feels just like old times."

"We will get back to how things were."

The smile faded from Whitton's face. "I don't think things will ever be like they were. I don't think they ever can be."

"I'm never going to stop waiting for you, you know," Smith said.

"I know. That's the problem. There's Bridge. I'll see you back at work."

She got out of the car and Smith watched her walk away.

* * *

Grant Webber and DI Smyth got out of Webber's car as soon as they saw Smith pull up to the kerb. Two men Smith knew to be part of Webber's team also got out.

"I left my phone at home," Smith told DI Smyth. "I was in such a rush after they let me out of the hospital. What's the plan?"

"We've spoken to a couple of the neighbours," DI Smyth said. "And none of them have seen Mr King for about a week, so we can assume he's not at home. Webber has kindly agreed for you to be present during the search."

"Get suited up first," the Head of Forensics said gruffly.

"I know the drill, Webber," Smith said.

"Can I have a word before we go in?" DI Smyth asked Smith.

He walked away from Robert King's house. Smith followed behind him.

"What's going on, boss?" Smith asked.

"I don't know what you heard this morning," the DI said.

"I don't follow you."

"You were outside Superintendent Smyth's office."

"I was on my way to my office," Smith argued.

"I may have only been here five minutes, but I've managed to get my bearings. Now, what did you hear?"

"I couldn't hear your conversation," Smith admitted. "The Super's door was closed, but I got the feeling you weren't planning a pleasant family get-together."

"I like you, DS Smith," DI Smyth said.

"You don't know me yet. In time you'll come to change your mind."

"Aside from your attitude yesterday," DI Smyth ignored Smith's flippancy. "Which I will put down to the effects of the migraine, you have shown me nothing but respect since my arrival here in York."

"You're a superior officer, boss. Respect is expected of me."

"I know all too well you've never associated respect with rank. With you, respect is based on ability and decision-making."

"I'll give you that," Smith said. "What *is* the story with you and the Super?"

"I'll tell you what the story is with me and Superintendent Smyth. If only to dispel speculation. Between you and me the man is a petty buffoon."

"I think you'll find that that opinion is not just shared between you and me, boss."

"But," DI Smyth's face turned serious. "Buffoon or not, he is still a Superintendent and he's not going anywhere. And getting back to the story between my uncle and I as you put it, it all started with a golfing holiday in Greece a few years back."

"I did hear the words, *golf* and *Greece* mentioned a few times," Smith admitted.

"I'm not a big fan of the game myself," DI Smyth said. "But my father and the Super have always been very keen. They set off for the course in high spirits. But when they returned after the game neither of them would talk to the other."

"Why not?" Smith asked. "What happened?"

"My father has a set of clubs he's particularly fond of, and he uses only that set of clubs. He transported them to Greece as he was planning on playing as much golf as possible there. Uncle Jeremy also had a favourite set."
Smith wasn't quite sure where the DI was going with this.
"After that particular round of golf when neither of them spoke, it finally transpired that the cause of the silent treatment was due to Uncle Jeremy mistaking my father's 9 iron for his own and subsequently refusing to give it back."
"You've got to be kidding me?" Smith had never heard of something so ridiculous in his life.
"I'm afraid not. And it gets worse. Uncle Jeremy to this day insists that 9 Iron is part of his set. They haven't spoken to each other since. That was three years ago."
"That is the most pathetic thing I've ever heard," Smith said.
"Isn't it just? I've tried to bang their heads together and make them see how petty it all is but they're both adamant. Until one of them admits they were wrong, the silent treatment will continue."
"Why are you telling me this?"
"Like I said," DI Smyth said. "To avoid speculation."
"What was the argument about today?" Smith asked. "Between you and the Super?"
"I was trying for the umpteenth time to make him see how ridiculous he and my father are being."
Smith shook his head. "Ridiculous is the right word. I assume this was after the Super had organised the warrant to search Robert King's house?"
"Of course. And speaking of which, we'd better get inside."

CHAPTER THIRTY TWO

Tim Darwin opened the door to Whitton and Bridge and frowned.

"Can I help you?"

"Police," Bridge showed him his ID. "DS Bridge and this is DC Whitton. Are you Tim Darwin?"

"I am. What's this all about?"

"We'd just like to ask you a few questions, Mr Darwin," Whitton told him. "Please can we come inside? It looks like it's going to rain."

They followed him inside. A child's bicycle was propped up just inside the door. Toys were strewn all over the hallway carpet.

"My son isn't the tidiest of kids," Tim explained. "But our teenage daughter's room is even worse. Come through."

Whitton and Bridge followed him through the last door on the right.

"What's going on?" Tim asked inside the living room. "Why do you want to talk to me?"

"We believe you're a member of the Greyham Rifle and Pistol Club," Whitton said. "Is that correct?"

"That's right. Why are you asking me about the club? Is this about the money that went missing? I've already been cleared of that. It was all a big misunderstanding."

"Mr Darwin," Bridge said. "We don't know anything about any missing money. This is about your shooting skills. We were told by the chairman that you are one of the top marksmen at the club."

"Billy?" Darwin looked shocked. "Did he really say that?"

"You seem surprised," Whitton said.

"Billy and me don't really get on. Does this have something to do with the recent shootings? I read about it online."

"Are you an active member of the club?" Whitton asked.

"I practise a couple of times a week. And I try to attend as many competitions as I can. Sometimes work gets in the way."

"What do you do for a living?" Bridge said.

"I'm a freelance photographer. I took all of these photographs."

He gestured to the walls in the room. Each one was covered with framed photos.

   Bridge stood up and walked over to one wall. "Where was this taken?" Tim moved closer and looked at the photo. It depicted four men – two of them with rifles and the other two holding scopes.

"That was during my time in Afghanistan. It was just after we won the inter-regiment event."

"Afghanistan?" Whitton said.

"I was stationed there at Camp Bastion. I got shot and was discharged. I never returned for a second term."

"You must have seen some pretty horrible stuff," Bridge said.

"It was quite dull most of the time," Tim said. "Ninety percent of the time was spent waiting around for something to happen. That's why we used to practise on the range so much."

"How did you end up getting shot?" Whitton asked.

"We came under heavy sniper fire one night in Musa Qala – the powers that be had underestimated the numbers of Taliban, and I was just unlucky. What has my time in Afghanistan got to do with the shootings in York?"

"We're not sure yet," Bridge said. "What rifle did you used to shoot with?"

"Arctic Warfare L96. It was the rifle of choice back in those days."

Whitton and Bridge looked at each other.

"Do you use the same rifle in the competitions here?" Bridge asked.

Tim started to laugh. "Of course not. They would never allow that in a civilian competition."

"So, what rifles do you use?"

"Why are you so interested in my rifles? Do you think I had something to do with the sniper killings? That's ridiculous – I haven't shot at anyone since I left Afghanistan."

"So, you have shot people before?" Whitton said.

"That was war, Constable. I was under orders to shoot people."

"How many rifles do you own, Mr Darwin?" Bridge could sense that his tone of voice was making Whitton quite angry.

"Just the three now," Tim replied. "I used to be something of a collector, but since the baby came along my wife insisted I sell most of them. I've got a Kimber Tactical, a MasterPiece Arms Lite PCR and a Daniel Defence DD5. That's my main competition rifle."

"We'll need to see them," Whitton said.

"What for?"

"Because we are also fighting a war out there, Mr Darwin. Where do you keep your rifles? I assume they are all locked away as per firearms regulations?"

Tim Darwin sighed. "Come with me."

He led them to a small conservatory attached to the side of the house. Against the wall stood a large metal cabinet. He took out a key and inserted it into one of two keyholes.

"I keep the key on me at all times."

He turned the key in the second lock and opened the door. He turned around and looked at Whitton.

"The cartridges are kept in a smaller safe upstairs in my study before you ask. As per firearms regulations."

"Could you take the rifles out, please," Whitton said.

"Do I need to call my lawyer?" Tim said and removed the nearest case from the cabinet.

"That's up to you," Whitton replied. "If you believe you require a legal representative, you are well within your rights to contact one. Which rifle is this?"

Tim Darwin had opened the first case.

"This is the Kimber."

He took out the next one.

"The MasterPiece needs a bit of work doing to the chassis. Some idiot dropped it at the range. And the last one is my favourite – the DD. Are you happy now?"

Bridge had seen photographs of the rifle used to kill four people in the past four days and none of the rifles in front of him looked remotely like it.

"Thank you," he said. "You can put them away again now."

Tim Darwin made no effort to hide his displeasure at having two detectives scrutinise his treasured rifles. He huffed and grunted while he replaced the weapons inside the cabinet.

He turned the key in the final lock. "Are you satisfied now? Can you leave me in peace?"

"I just want to take a look at something again," Bridge said.

He made his way back to the living room before Tim Darwin had a chance to argue. Whitton found him staring at the same photograph he'd been looking at earlier.

"What are you thinking?" she asked him.

"This is definitely the same rifle on the photos Webber showed us," Bridge said. "I just wanted to double check."

"Is it time to make that phone call to my lawyer now?" Tim Darwin had come inside the room. "I believe police harassment charges are taken quite seriously these days."

"We're finished here," Bridge said. "Who are the people in this photograph?"

Darwin didn't even have to look at it. "That's me on the left with my spotter, Dave. The spotter next to Dave is some bloke everybody called Welly and the other sniper next to him is Rob King."

CHAPTER THIRTY THREE

Grant Webber turned the key Robert King's landlord had given them and turned to look at Smith.

"I know," Smith got there first. "I won't touch anything or move anything around. I'm suited up for Pete's sake."

Webber didn't say anything further. He pushed the front door open and went inside. Two of his technicians followed him and Smith and DI Smyth brought up the rear. Two PCs stood sentry outside the front door. Dark clouds were merging together in the sky above them at an alarming rate. Rain was inevitable. Suddenly, a high-pitched wailing noise was heard. It seemed to get louder the longer it screeched.

"Damn it," Webber had to shout over the alarm. "The security company was supposed to have disarmed the alarm."

"Get hold of them," Smith screamed.

"No need," Webber pointed to the van that was driving towards them.

A white transit van drove up and parked behind Smith's car. On the side of the van was a logo: *Stay Well Security*. Two men got out and walked up the path towards them.

"What's going on?" the shorter of the two asked.

The alarm was still blaring.

"Police," Smith showed him his ID. "We need to go inside. This alarm was supposed to have been disarmed."

"Hold on." The short man took out his mobile phone and walked away. He returned a short time later, and soon the street was silent.

"Slight glitch in the system," he told Smith. "I'll leave you to it."

"Let's start again, shall we?" Webber said.

"What exactly are we looking for?" Smith heard one of Webber's team ask.

"You'll know when you find it," was the Head of Forensics' reply.

Smith headed down the hall. The SOC suit was incredibly uncomfortable and it was already beginning to make him itch. He went inside the kitchen and was surprised at how clean it was. There were no dirty dishes in the sink and every surface was spotless.

"He's obviously a bit of a neat-freak," he said to DI Smyth.

"Army does that to you," the DI explained. "It's hard to break the habit when you've been used to that kind of discipline."

Smith began opening the cupboards but found nothing that shouldn't be there. Pots, pans, plastic containers and other normal items that most kitchens contain were all he found.

"You were in the army," Smith said. "If this was your house, where would you keep a gun safe?"

"I was in intelligence," DI Smyth reminded him. "I think I've probably shot a gun two or three times, but if I was to hide a gun safe somewhere it would be somewhere nobody would think a gun safe would be."

"The bathroom, you mean?"

"Don't be ridiculous. I'd hide it somewhere in plain sight. Somewhere really obvious. Look around this room. What do you see?"

Smith did just that. It was a relatively large kitchen with a central working area and ample space to move around in. There was a washing machine and a tumble drier against one wall and on the other side there was a double stainless-steel sink. Next to the sink was a large fridge. And next to the fridge was a chest freezer.

"Why does a single man need a chest freezer?" Smith asked. "That fridge has a huge freezer compartment."

He tried the door of the fridge. It opened and Smith closed it when he saw that all it contained was a carton of milk and some mouldy cheese. He tried the door on the freezer.

It was locked.

Grant Webber came in. "We didn't find anything upstairs. There's a gun safe we managed to open with a crowbar but all it contained was a couple of ordinary competition rifles. No Arctic L96's."

"What do you think of this freezer?" Smith said.

Webber took a closer look. "It's a freezer. What do you want me to say?"

"Don't you think it's odd that a man who lives on his own has two freezers?"

"Not really. Maybe he's a food addict. Maybe he keeps his food in a separate freezer."

"Let's find out," Smith said. "Where's that crowbar?"

It took Webber's technician less than a minute to break the lock on Robert King's freezer. Webber placed his hand on the door and yanked it open.

"My God," he stepped back.

"What is it?" Smith asked.

"Well, it appears that the Arctic Warfare L96 lives up to its reputation as an extreme weather rifle," Webber said. "It appears to have survived being kept in a refrigerator."

He removed the rifle. Behind it was a telescopic scope and a night optic. Webber took these out as well.

"There's a load of loose cartridges in here too."

He took out an uncovered box full of the 51mm Winchester Magnum ammunition.

"This is unbelievable," DI Smyth said.

"It was your call, boss," Smith told him. "You're the one who insisted on the search warrant. Not bad in your first week."

Webber carried on emptying the contents of the fridge.

"Would you look at this?"

He removed another telescopic sight.

"This is a Schmidt and Bender PM series sight. It's strictly military issue."

"Whatever you say, Webber," Smith said.

"It has a laser filter," Webber elaborated. "And what do we have here?"

"What is it?" DI Smyth asked.

"It's the reason why we didn't find anything at the suspected shooting sites." Webber leaned inside the fridge and took out four empty cartridge cases.

"I'd say this one is done and dusted. Case closed."

"We still need to find the bloke," Smith reminded him. "He's disappeared in case you've forgotten."

"At least there's not going to be any more shooting," Webber said. "That's one thing."

"Sir," one of the PC's had come inside the kitchen.

"What is it?" Smith said.

"Someone's just pulled into the driveway, sir."

Smith left the room and walked towards the front door. He went outside and was hit in the face by a blast of rain. The wind died for a second and then the heavens opened. Smith stepped back inside the doorway. A blue hatchback was parked in the drive. A tall, balding man got out and ran towards him.

"What the hell are you doing in my house?" he said to Smith.

"Who are you?" Smith asked him.

"Robert King," he replied. "This is my house."

CHAPTER THIRTY FOUR

"Interview with Robert King commenced, 13:15," DI Smyth said. "Present DI Smyth and DS Smith and Hilary Hayes, Mr King's legal representation. Mr King do you understand why you are here?"

"I have no bloody idea," King said.

"Mr King," Hilary said. "Please watch your language."

"Well it's true," King glared at her. "I come home after a lovely week in the Lakes to find the house full of coppers and then I'm arrested for murder. Would you watch your language if it was you?"

"OK," Smith interrupted. "Mr King, you are aware that we found an army-issue sniper rifle in a freezer in your kitchen. Can you please explain how it got there?"

"You tell me."

"You're going to have to do better than that," DI Smyth said.

"How?" King raised his voice. "How am I supposed to tell you where it came from when I have no fucking idea myself?"

"Mr King," Hilary said sternly.

"I do not know what that L96 was doing in my freezer," King said.

"Are you familiar with the Arctic L96?"

"It was the rifle I trained with."

"Where was this?"

"I toured in Afghanistan," King looked Smith directly in the eyes. "I got shot at by the fucking Taliban, defending your arse, and this is what I get for it. This is totally fucking ridiculous."

"Mr King," Hilary raised her voice.

"It's OK, Mrs Hayes," DI Smyth said. "If he wants to express himself, let him."

"Can you tell us about your time in Afghanistan?" Smith asked.

DI Smyth nodded to him in approval.

"I did a tour there from 2005 to 2009. What else is there to say?"

"What was your role there?" DI Smyth said.

"I was trained as a sniper."

"And what did that entail?"

"What do you think it entailed? I shot enemy soldiers."

"Would you consider yourself a good marksman?" Smith asked.

"I've been told as much. I killed people in Afghanistan – we were fighting a fucking war. I did not kill civilians."

"OK," Smith said. "You were married to Wendy Price, weren't you?"

"That bitch," King said.

"Go on."

"While I was thousands of miles away dodging bullets, that bitch starts shagging another bloke. She told me in a letter. Can you believe it? A fucking letter."

"She's dead, Mr King," DI Smyth informed him.

"What?"

"She's dead. She was gunned down on Sunday afternoon outside a supermarket. She was killed with a bullet from an Arctic L96."

King remained silent.

"She was shot from a distance of around six-hundred metres, Mr King," Smith said after a moment. "That's quite a shot to make, wouldn't you say?"

"I didn't kill Wendy," King said. "Why would I do that?"

"Do you know Charles Lincoln?" Smith decided to change tack.

"No."

"What about Diana Wells? Or Liam Lovelake?"

King shook his head.

"For the record, Mr King is shaking his head," DI Smyth said. "Mr King, where have you been for the past week? Your place of work told us you haven't been at work since Monday last week, and none of your neighbours have seen you at home. Where were you?"

"I was in the Lakes," King said. "I've already told you that."

"Can anybody confirm this?"

"Probably not. I was up in the Fells camping. I like to be away from the crowds."

"So," Smith said. "Are you not aware of the recent shootings? It's been all over the news."

"Are you fucking deaf?"

"Mr King," Hilary Hayes said.

Smith held his hand up to indicate it was OK.

"I just told you I was up in the Fells," King said. "No phone reception, therefore, no news. Do you get it now? Can I get something to drink? Or is that too much to fucking ask?"

"Of course not," DI Smyth said. "Interview with Robert King paused, 13:34."

"What do you think?" DI Smyth asked Smith in the corridor outside the interview room.

Robert King had been given twenty minutes to consult with his legal representative. Two uniformed officers stood outside the room.

"I think he needs to work on his vocabulary. Is that how people really talk in the military?"

"Not all of us."

His mobile phone started to ring.

"Smyth," he answered it.

Smith watched as the DI listened. After a minute he ended the call.

"That was Webber," he told Smith. "He didn't find any prints on the rifle, but he's confirmed that the cartridges pulled from all four murders were fired from the rifle we found in his kitchen. We've got him."

"I still don't get it," Smith said. "Why kill all those other people? Sure, he's pissed off with his ex-wife, but why kill the others?"

"Let's go and find out, shall we?"

CHAPTER THIRTY FIVE

A few hundred metres away from Robert King's house, a man dressed all in black was smiling. He packed the telescopic scope away in its case and walked towards his car. He'd watched the whole thing, and he couldn't believe the series of events. It was as though divine intervention had been on his side. It was as if it was destined to happen this way.
Karma, you could call it.

The man had watched as the police went inside the house. Two uniformed officers stood outside the whole time. The rain had started to fall. A while later a blue car had parked outside and Robert King got out. King had changed a lot since the last time the man had seen him. His hairline had receded greatly, and he had lines on his face that hadn't been there before. The only thing that hadn't changed were his eyes.
Those eyes that always seemed to promise malice.

The wind was now blowing in gusts and the scope was becoming misted up. The man had wiped the lens just in time to see the haunted-looking policeman emerge from the house. Robert King had approached him and a short while later he was taken away. It had all worked out perfectly, and now King would get what he deserved. Even Robert King wouldn't be able to talk his way out of this.

* * *

"Interview with Robert King recommenced, 13:55," DI Smyth said. "Mr King, is there anything you'd like to say?"
"No comment."
Smith was worried this might happen. After his consultation with his legal representative, King had obviously been advised not to say anything further.
"What is it you don't have a comment about?" he said.
"What?"

"Mr King," DI Smyth said. "We've just had it confirmed – the rifle we found in your freezer was the one used to kill four people. Surely you'd like to comment on that?"

"I have no fucking idea what you're talking about," King said. "That freezer was empty when I left last week."

"Why do you have two freezers?" Smith asked him.

"I use it for my venison."

"Deer?" Smith said.

"I can see why they made you a detective."

"Why is it empty?" Smith said.

"Because the hunting season hasn't started yet. I'll be heading up to Scotland in a couple of weeks and hopefully I'll have a couple of carcasses to bring back."

"So, you still maintain you have no idea how that rifle ended up in your freezer?"

"No comment," Hilary Hayes spoke for her client.

"There's one thing I don't understand," Smith said. "When we searched your house earlier, we were met with an alarm that could wake the dead. If what you're implying is true and someone else put that rifle in your meat freezer, how did they get past the alarm?"

"No comment," King said.

   "Mr King," Smith said. "Let me tell you how this looks from where I'm sitting. We have four dead people, one of whom happens to be your ex-wife. An ex-wife you've already called a bitch on tape. These four people were killed with the same firearm we discovered in your kitchen. The killings were undertaken with absolute precision. Very few people are able to shoot a rifle like this. Can you see how this looks for you?"

"No comment."

"There's just one thing I'd like to know before we charge you with four counts of murder," Smith said. "Your wife I can understand – you hated the way she betrayed you, but why kill the others? Why did three innocent people have to die? Wendy was the third victim. What's the story with the others? Were they mere sacrifices to throw us off the scent? Was that why you didn't just shoot your ex? Because that would have looked suspicious wouldn't it?"

A faint spark of something like recognition appeared in Robert King's eyes. "What did you say?"

"Was that your plan?" Smith said. "Your ex was the main target, but you knew you'd be the main suspect if she was the only one, so you made her the third victim to confuse us."

"That was my plan," King said.

"Now we're getting somewhere," DI Smyth said. "Go on."

"But that's all it was," King seemed quite animated now. "A plan, nothing more. I could never have carried it out."

"What are you talking about?" Smith asked him.

"After I got the letter from Wendy," King continued. "The one telling me about this Russian millionaire she'd started shagging, I hatched a plan to get rid of her. But it was nothing more than a plot for a perfect murder. I promise you."

"And what exactly was this plot for a perfect murder?" DI Smyth said.

"You kill people with a sniper rifle. There's one person you want to kill but you don't just kill them because then the shadow of guilt would fall straight on you. So, you make the intended victim the second or third victim then the police will think the victims are connected somehow. And for good measure you shoot someone else even after you've killed the person you want to kill. It was just an idea I came up with in Afghanistan."

"It is an excellent plan," Smith agreed. "And it nearly worked for you didn't it?"

"I didn't kill those people."

King looked at his solicitor. "I didn't do this."

"Mr King," DI Smyth said. "We have more than enough to hold you in custody for seventy-two hours while we decide whether we've got strong enough grounds to charge you. I have to warn you that in all probability you will be charged with all four counts of murder, so I suggest you use that time to do some thinking. Interview with Robert King ended, 14:10."

He switched off the recording device.

"You will be escorted into custody," DI Smyth told King.

He and Smith stood up and headed for the door. Hilary Hayes remained behind with her client.

"Tim Darwin," King shouted when Smith and DI Smyth were outside in the corridor.

Smith came back into the interview room. "What did you say?"

"Tim Darwin," King said again. "I told him my plan."

"What are you suggesting, Mr King?"

"Darwin hated me," King said. "He didn't let on, but he blamed me for him getting shot. He thinks I did it on purpose, but I didn't. I was just too late. It all makes sense. Darwin carried out my plan to frame me."

"Good bye, Mr King," Smith said and walked back outside the room.

CHAPTER THIRTY SIX

"That's that then," DI Smyth said.

He and Smith sat in the canteen. Smith looked out of the window at the rain pelting against the glass. A familiar feeling was building inside his stomach – it was the feeling he got when something wasn't right. He took a sip of his coffee and winced. It was still boiling hot.

"Something doesn't add up."

DI Smyth looked at him. "What are you trying to say?"

"It just seems too easy that's all. Four people are dead – they were killed without the killer even being at the scene, and now we have the murderer in custody. After four days. Something doesn't add up."

"It was outstanding detective work," DI Smyth said. "That's all there is to it."

"No," Smith shook his head. "No investigation has ever been this easy. It's all wrong."

"In my experience sometimes a bit of luck helps in an investigation. This was one of those times. We got a bit of luck."

"Or a bit of help," Smith thought out loud. "That's what it feels like to me – somebody helped us catch Rob King."

"Are you saying somebody framed him?"

"I don't know," Smith stood up. "But I'm not going to be celebrating just yet."

"I've called a briefing at three. Or a debriefing if you like. You can debate whether Robert King is our killer all you like, but all the evidence points directly to him. I don't think I've ever seen so much damning evidence."

"Exactly," Smith said and walked away.

His coffee sat steaming on the table.

He headed outside for a cigarette. The rain had died down to a drizzle, but the wind was still howling. Smith made his way round the back of the building where it was more sheltered. DCI Chalmers was standing there smoking.

"Great minds think alike," Chalmers said. "I believe congratulations are in order."

"Boss?" Smith took out his cigarettes, lit one and inhaled deeply.

"I heard you've got a suspect in custody for the recent shootings. Great work. DI Smyth seems to have started with a bang."

"I'm not sure, boss," Smith said, exhaling a huge cloud of smoke. "Something about the whole thing doesn't feel right."

"It never does with you. What's wrong now?"

"It was too easy if that makes sense. We've got a man who meticulously plans four murders and carries them all out with absolute precision and we end up catching him because he's got the murder weapon hidden in a freezer in his kitchen."

"So, he slipped up," Chalmers said. "The bloke probably didn't expect us to come looking."

"I don't buy it. If Robert King is our man, he *would* have expected us to come looking. There are very few people around with his particular skills – he would have known we'd want to speak to him sooner or later."

"How's it going with Smyth's nephew?" Chalmers changed the subject.

"He's actually a good DI," Smith admitted. "And not what I expected at all."

"I told you. And he's been saying good things about you."

"Really?"

"I don't want to add air to your already over-inflated ego, but one of the reasons he came to York was to be able to work alongside you. He could have gone anywhere he wanted with his credentials."

"That'll be a first. I'd better get back in – the DI has called a briefing in light of the recent developments. He actually called it a debriefing."

"Army speak," Chalmers threw his cigarette on the ground and stood on it. "Stop being so hard on yourself. Enjoy the success for once."

Chalmers' words hadn't worked. Smith still had a niggling feeling that something about Robert King didn't fit. He headed for the small conference room and had just reached the front desk when he spotted something out of the corner of his eye. He turned to see what it was but whatever it was remained in the corner of his eye. It was a blurry light. No matter where he looked the light stayed where it was. He tried to blink it away, but it didn't work. A dull pain had now made its way from his forehead and had settled over his left eye. The light in his peripheral vision had intensified and was now flashing with a greater intensity.

I'm having a migraine attack, Smith thought.

He cursed himself for leaving the medication at home. He approached the front desk and tried to focus on the face manning the desk. The flashing light had now blocked out the sight in his left eye.

"I need painkillers," he said to the PC. "Anything. Paracetamol, Aspirin, Ibuprofen, anything."

"Sir?" the PC looked at him strangely.

"I'm having a migraine attack," Smith told him. "Have you got any painkillers behind the desk?"

"No, sir. I'll go and see if I can find some."

Smith couldn't hear him. His whole head was now throbbing with pain and it felt like his left eyeball was going to explode. He managed to make his way to the row of chairs opposite the front desk and he sat down.

"Are you alright?" It was Whitton.

Smith looked up at her. Her face appeared to be moving backwards and forwards and he winced as an intense pain shot through his head.

The PC who had been manning the desk appeared behind Whitton. To Smith they appeared to have merged into one blurred figure. The part of the figure that was Whitton put two white tablets in Smith's hand and spoke. Smith couldn't make out the words she was saying. He breathed in deeply and glanced at the tablets in his hand. Blackness had engulfed the vision in his left eye, but his right eye registered what he had in his hand. He managed to swallow the tablets and take a sip of water from the cup Whitton handed him.

Smith felt a hand on his forehead. The throbbing had been replaced by a dull ache and the vision was slowly returning to his left eye. Whitton was sitting next to him by the front desk. Bridge and Yang Chu looked on, concerned.

"Are you alright?" Whitton left her hand on his forehead.
Smith didn't know why he did what he did next.
He turned so he was facing her, leaned forward and kissed his wife on the lips. She didn't pull away. They stayed as they were for a few seconds then Whitton carefully placed Smith's head on her shoulder.
"I'll take you home," she said and stroked his hair. "You shouldn't be driving so I'll give you a lift."
"What time is it?" Smith spoke into her shoulder.
He breathed in deeply and closed his eyes. Her scent brought back everything he'd lost – everything he'd thrown away.
"It's almost five," Whitton told him. "You've been here by the front desk for almost two hours. How are you feeling?"
"Much better now. I missed the briefing."
"Don't worry about that now. You'll find out about it in the morning. Let's get you home."
Smith didn't argue. He let himself be helped to his feet and walked out of the station.

CHAPTER THIRTY SEVEN

Smith watched as Whitton's car drove off down the street. He'd asked her to come inside but she'd declined. Smith thought about the kiss, smiled and winced as a wave of pain hit his forehead. He made a mental note to make sure he always carried some pain medication with him from now on. He went inside his house and let the dogs in. The two boys were nowhere near as boisterous as they usually were when let inside – it was as though they sensed there was something wrong with Smith.
"I had another migraine," he told them and filled their bowls with food. "It's not something I would wish on anybody."
The dogs weren't paying attention. Filling their bellies was taking precedence over Smith's ailments.
Fred finished first for a change.

Smith realised he hadn't eaten anything all day. It was becoming a habit. He wasn't particularly hungry, but he forced down some boiled eggs on toast. He headed outside for a smoke. Thankfully the rain clouds had drifted off to the west, but a new bank was slowly moving towards him in the distance. He lit a cigarette and tried to think about what had happened that day. He couldn't concentrate – his thoughts were incoherent, and he found it difficult to concentrate on anything for more than a few seconds. He admitted defeat, stubbed out his cigarette and went back inside.

After a quick shower, Smith felt much better. He switched on his PC and made some coffee while he waited for it to boot up. When it was ready Smith typed *migraine* in the search bar. If he was going to suffer attacks, he wanted to make sure he knew everything there was to know about them. He clicked on the first link and started reading. According to this particular health site, migraines were a relative enigma in the medical world. There was no concrete proof as to what exactly causes them but the general consensus is, they are hereditary. Smith tried to think back. Had his mother or father suffered from them? He couldn't remember.

He read further and discovered that the particular migraine he suffered from was known as a Classic Migraine and it was extremely rare. Reading further Smith shook his head when he saw what the most common triggers for an attack were.

Stress, caffeine and skipping meals.

He could count all three as major aspects of his lifestyle.

Nothing else on the site gave him anything more than he already knew so he closed down the page and shut down his PC. He made up his mind he would just have to grin and bear his new ailment and try and recognise the warning signs. And he would make sure he always carried his medication with him. He smoked another cigarette and made another cup of coffee.

Smith had just turned on the television when his doorbell rang. He got up and went to see who it was. Whitton was standing on the doorstep. She was holding a carrier bag from a takeaway.

"You don't have to ring the bell," Smith told her. "This is still your house."

"I know," Whitton said. "But it would have felt odd just walking in. Are you hungry?"

"Is that Chinese?"

"It is."

"Then I'm hungry. Come in and prepare yourself for an onslaught. Those dogs are going to go crazy."

That was an understatement. As soon as Whitton set foot inside the kitchen Theakston and Fred went wild. The Chubby Bull Terrier and the grotesque Pug began by running in circles around her. Theakston jumped up at her legs and almost sent her flying.

"That's enough, boys," Smith said, but the dogs ignored him.

Whitton started to laugh. "I don't know if it's me they're excited about or the takeaway."

"Definitely the takeaway," Smith said. "I'll get us some plates."

"How's the headache?" Whitton asked when they'd finished.

Smith had managed to eat more than he expected.

"It's much better now. Whatever those pills were seemed to have worked. What did that PC give me anyway?"

"He found some over-the-counter paracetamol. I thought you were told to keep some pain killers on you at all times."

"I left them at home. It's nice having you at home again."

"I'm not exactly *at home*," Whitton told him. "I just came to see how you were – I was worried about you."

"That's something at least."

"I want to talk about it."

"Talk about what?"

"That night," Whitton said. "I want you to tell me about that night – I want to try and understand."

"Are you sure?"

"I'm here aren't I?"

"Where would you like me to start?" Smith asked.

"Just tell me what happened that night."

Smith thought hard. He thought about that night when he bumped into PC Baldwin at the Hog's Head.

"We'd had a fight," he told Whitton. "Not so much a fight, but I was pretty rude to you in the briefing and you stormed out of the room. I remember I got quite a bollocking from Chalmers for the way I spoke to you. And I also remember thinking that just because you were my wife didn't mean I had to treat you any differently to anyone else on the team."

"You mean you can be as rude as you like to all of us?" Whitton said.

"I didn't mean it like that. Anyway, the whole way home I was mad. I realise now that I was more mad at myself than you. I got home and tried to phone you, but you didn't answer. I waited a while and tried again. When you didn't reply I assumed you were avoiding me and that just made me angrier. I went to the Hog's Head and that's where I met Baldwin."

"What was she doing there in the first place?" Whitton asked. "She doesn't normally go to the Hog's Head."

"I don't know. I really don't know. We had a bite to eat and quite a few drinks and we spoke about the Demons case. I remember thinking that her insight was refreshing. We'd been banging our heads up against a brick wall and Baldwin was the only one who actually understood where I was coming from."

"I see," Whitton said calmly.

"It was getting late, so I offered to walk her home. I'd had quite a bit to drink and I had a sort of temporary blackout. I joked that I needed coffee and somehow, I ended up in Baldwin's flat. She made the coffee and I remember we could hear sirens in the distance. I didn't know that they were on their way to the accident you were involved in."

"What happened then?" Whitton wiped a tear from the corner of her eye.

"Do you really want to hear this?"

"I told you, I want to try and understand."

"To be honest I don't actually remember how it happened. We were still talking, we ended up closer together and the next thing I know, we're kissing each other. I did not plan for that to happen. You have to believe me."

Whitton remained silent. More tears were now flowing from her eyes.

"I am so sorry," Smith placed his hand on her shoulder. "I really am sorry."

"I can't do this," Whitton brushed his hand away. "I thought I could, but I can't."

"I will do anything it takes to have you back in my life," Smith told her. "Anything you want."

"I know," Whitton raised her voice. "And I want to believe you but how can I believe you when I can't trust you? I'm not sure I'll ever be able to trust you ever again."

"I'll wait as long as it takes. I want you and Laura back here."

"I have to go," Whitton stood up, picked up her car keys and left without saying another word.

CHAPTER THIRTY EIGHT

"Let's get started," DI Smyth said. "We have a lot to get through. Robert King isn't budging. He still claims he had nothing to do with the murders of those four people. Therefore, we need to start building a watertight case against him. The Crown Prosecution Service will want concrete proof before charges can be brought, and I believe we have more than enough to secure a conviction."

"Something doesn't feel right about King," Smith said.

Everybody in the room turned to look at him.

"Why do you have to always throw a spanner in the works?" It was Bridge. "Every time we're about to put a case to bed, you always have to question it."

"And how has that worked for me in the past?" Smith said.

Bridge didn't reply to this. He knew that Smith had a valid point.

"What is your problem?" DI Smyth said. "We've got an experienced marksman who just happened to have our murder weapon in his house. What exactly do you want? A signed confession in blood?"

"King said something in the interview yesterday," Smith said. "And it's something we have to look into."

"Do you want to refresh my memory?" DI Smyth was clearly getting quite irritated.

"He spoke about a plot for a perfect murder. And the more I think about it the more it makes sense."

He had the attention of everybody in the room now.

"Let's say you want to kill someone," Smith said. "But you realise that you will automatically be regarded as the number one suspect by doing so. So, you confuse matters by making it look like a series of murders rather than one single hit."

"You're confusing the hell out of me right now," Bridge chipped in.

"Just hear me out. Wendy Price was the third victim. Before her there was Charles Lincoln and Diana Wells. What do we do first when we have a series of murders?"

"We try and find a link between the victims," Whitton joined in.

Smith smiled at her. She didn't smile back.

"Exactly. And that takes up a lot of time. What if the killer knew that's how we operate? He makes it look like a string of murders yet really there is only one *intended* victim."

"That sounds a bit far-fetched to me," Yang Chu said.

"I agree," Smith said. "And yesterday I would have thought the same thing but after speaking to Robert King it didn't seem so ridiculous. King outlined the plan he'd come up with and it fitted perfectly with how these killings were carried out."

"But if he did come up with this plan," Bridge said. "Why do we need to dig any further? Surely what he said was as close to a confession as we need."

"That brings me to my next point," Smith said. "What if the plot for the perfect murder was taken one step further? King mentioned Tim Darwin. He and Darwin served together in Afghanistan and Darwin is the only person he told about this plan. Darwin blamed King for letting him get shot, so what if Darwin used King's plan against him? He carries out the plan and implicates King in doing so. You have to agree, it is rather ingenious."

"I think that migraine yesterday has addled your brain," Bridge said.

Smith patted the pocket of his jeans. The two tablets were still there.

"What harm can it do to go and have another chat with Tim Darwin?" Smith said.

"What exactly are you going to say to him?" DI Smyth asked.

"I'm not going to directly accuse him of four murders," Smith said. "I'm going to see if he lets anything slip without realising it."

"I still think it's a waste of time," Bridge was adamant. "King is our man. Plain and simple."

"It is a loose end that needs tying up," Smith told him.

"OK," Smyth said. "I suppose it can't do any harm. Smith, you and Whitton go and have a chat with Darwin. In the meantime, I want to have another crack at Robert King. Maybe a night in the cells will have made him more willing to talk. Bridge, you can sit in with me."

* * *

"Are you alright?" Smith asked Whitton as they drove to the Greyham Rifle and Pistol Club.

Tim Darwin's wife had told them that's where they would find him.

"I'm fine," Whitton said.

"I'm sorry about last night."

"I asked for it. I asked you to tell me what happened. It was a mistake."

"I don't know what to do, Erica. Tell me what to do and I'll do it."

"I don't know what I want you to do," Whitton admitted. "That's the problem. I tried to believe I could put it behind us but it's not that easy – it's always there in the back of my head, lingering like a bad dream."

"I just want to be near you," Smith said. "That's all I need. Just to know you're still there somewhere close."

"I still need time. You seem pretty sure about this Tim Darwin bloke."

"I'm not sure," Smith admitted. "But I've got a strong feeling that Robert King didn't do this. It seems all too convenient to me."

"You mean it stinks of a frame-up?"

"Exactly. You do not go to all the trouble of planning and carrying out four precision murders and then get busted because you leave the murder weapon in your kitchen. It's just not right."

He turned left and joined the dual carriageway.

"We should go away," he said

"What?"

"We should get away for a few days."

"Like a holiday?"

"Yes. Just you, me and Laura. We don't have to go far. And we don't have to share the same room if you don't want to."

"I want that more than anything," Whitton said. "I miss you like crazy, but I'm scared to let you back in."

"A holiday is just what we need. After this is all over."

CHAPTER THIRTY NINE

Smith parked in the car park next to the rifle club and he and Whitton got out of the car.

"I still can't understand why people would want to do this as a hobby," he said. "Guns are not something you play around with."

"They have shooting in the Olympics," Whitton informed him. "It's quite a popular sport."

"What's wrong with a simple game of football?" Smith said. "And I hate football."

"Darwin's wife said that Billy Forest should be here," Whitton said. "She said the Chairman of the club is always around."

They found him as soon as they walked through the front doors. He was speaking on his mobile phone by the front desk. Smith waited for him to end the call and approached him.

"Morning," Smith said. "We're looking for Tim Darwin. His wife told us he would be here."

"He's been out on the range since early this morning," Billy told them. "We've got a big competition coming up and Tim wants to make sure he's as sharp as possible for it."

Smith remembered something Whitton told him Tim Darwin had said the last time they spoke. Darwin seemed surprised when Whitton told him that Billy Forest reckoned he was one of the best marksmen at the club. Tim had mentioned something about him and Billy not always seeing eye to eye.

"Mr Forest," Smith said. "Before we speak to Mr Darwin there's something I need to ask you."

"Go ahead," Billy said. "I'm just about finished up here anyway."

"What do you think of Tim Darwin?"

"He's one of the best marksmen I've ever seen. I believe I've already told you that."

"I don't mean as a marksman, what do you think of Tim as a person?"

"Why are you asking me that?"

"Please, Mr Forest, just answer the question."

"Well, we're not friends," Billy admitted. "And we don't always agree on certain things."

"What do you mean?"

"Let's just say I think there's a lot more to Tim Darwin than meets the eye."

"Are you talking about the missing money?" Whitton came straight out with it.

"How do you know about that?"

"Mr Darwin told us," Smith said. "What exactly happened?"

"It was a while ago," Billy looked around the room as though he was afraid they were being overheard. "Tim was acting as secretary for the club. I happened to check the accounts one day and realised there was money missing - money that couldn't be accounted for."

"Did you confront Mr Darwin about this?" Whitton asked.

"Of course I did. I'm the chairman of the club and therefore the buck stops at me. I would have been held accountable."

"So, what happened then?" Smith said.

"Tim denied it of course," Billy continued. "He said I'd made a mistake."

"How much money are we talking about here?"

"Not a substantial amount – a thousand pounds more or less."

"What did you believe Mr Darwin intended to do with the money?" Whitton said.

"I have no idea, and I'll never find out. The very next week the money was back in the account and the matter was never brought up again. Tim resigned from the secretary position soon after."

"Thank you, Mr Forest," Billy said. "One more thing, what are your thoughts on Robert King?"

"Rob?" Billy laughed. "What does anyone think about Rob? He can be the life and soul of a party one minute and an out and out bastard the next."

"What do you mean?" Whitton said.

"Let's just say when Rob's in a good mood he can charm the pants off anybody, but God help anybody who crosses him. He has a real nasty streak in him."

"We won't take up anymore of your time," Smith said.

Tim Darwin was taking a break on a bench in front of the range. He spotted Smith and Whitton and frowned.

"What do you lot want now?" he asked when they got nearer. "Didn't you put me through enough last time?"

"Apparently not," Smith said. "How's the shooting going?"

"It was going great until you showed up. What do you want?"

"Are you aware that Robert King has been arrested for the recent shootings in the city?" Smith asked him.

"What?" Tim's face displayed genuine surprise. "You can't possibly think Rob had anything to do with it. That's ridiculous."

"Why is that?" Whitton asked him.

"It just is. Rob wouldn't shoot anyone.

"He shot plenty of people in Afghanistan," Whitton reminded him.

"That was different," Tim's eyes darkened. "I told you, we were fighting a war."

"One of the victims was Mr King's ex-wife," Smith said. "Did you know her?"

"No. I heard about her – Rob received the Dear John letter while we were at Camp Bastion, but I never met the woman. Why are you asking me about all of this?"

"What was your relationship with Mr King like in Afghanistan?" Whitton asked.

"I wouldn't say we were friends, but we were on the same side, so we had to try and get along."

"You didn't tell us that Mr King was with you the night you got shot," Smith said.

"You didn't ask. What is this really about?"

"When we spoke to Mr King yesterday he told us something interesting. You were under heavy sniper fire that night in Musa Qala, weren't you?"

"It was worse than usual," Tim admitted.

"And you and Mr King were tasked with clearing the hills opposite?"

"We'd taken cover behind one of the armed vehicles, and we were picking them off one by one. I spotted movement halfway up the embankment and when I got a closer look, I realised it was kids shooting at us. I'd just found out that my wife was expecting and maybe that was why, but I just couldn't bring myself to shoot children."

He became quiet for a moment and a pained expression appeared on his face.

"What happened next, Mr Darwin?" Whitton urged.

"Rob screamed at me to shoot and I told him I couldn't – they were kids. He told me there were no kids out here, only Taliban soldiers and he shot them both in quick succession."

"Is that why you got shot?" Smith asked.

"No. There was this one sniper dressed all in black, and I spotted him too late. Rob was a split second too late, too and I got shot before Rob put him down. What has all of this got to do with Rob's arrest?"

"Mr King believes you blame him for getting shot," Smith said. "He is under the impression that you think he held off shooting this man in black deliberately."

"I did at the time," Tim admitted. "But it was chaos out there and I wasn't thinking straight. Rob and me are all good now. Like I said, we'll never be close friends but we're civil to one another. I still don't understand why you're here."

Tim Darwin looked at Whitton and then at Smith.

"Hold on. Do you think I had something to do with these shootings? Is that what this is all about?"

"We need to know your whereabouts on these dates," Smith told him the dates and approximate times the shootings occurred.

"I think I'd better contact my lawyer," Tim said. "And that police harassment charge is looking more and more probable."

"If you can just tell us where you were on those dates, we can corroborate it and eliminate you from our enquiries," Smith told him. "It's as simple as that."

Tim scratched his head. "Last Friday, you said?"

"That was the first one, yes. Around eight in the morning."

"I was at home."

"Can anyone vouch for you?" Whitton asked.

"I was there alone. My wife took our son to daycare at ten-to and returned just after ten."

"So, you were alone for two hours?" Smith said.

"I did not kill those people."

"What about the other dates and times?" Whitton reminded him of them.

"Not until I've spoken to my lawyer. If you're going to persist with these ridiculous claims, I'm going to need someone on my side."

"That's your legal right," Smith said. "We'll set up a formal interview. I assume you can be trusted to make your way to the station off your own bat?"

"I'll be there," Tim smiled defiantly. "And I assure you, you're making a huge mistake here."

"It's a bad habit of mine," Smith said. "We'll be in touch. There is just one more question I'd like to know the answer to."

"Not without my lawyer present."

"Suit yourself. I'll ask it anyway – what did you do with the money you stole from the club's bank account?"

Smith and Whitton walked away, leaving a wide-mouthed Tim Darwin in their wake.

CHAPTER FORTY

"You're terrible," Whitton said as Smith turned right onto the main road heading back towards the city.

"I just thought I'd rattle him a bit," he said.

"Do you think he's involved?"

"I don't know – usually when an innocent person is asked where they were at a certain time, they're only too happy to provide us with an alibi, unless they don't have one. We'll see what we get out of him in a formal interview."

"What happens if the CPS decides we have enough to charge Robert King? Doesn't that complicate matters?"

"Not at all," Smith said. "If King is charged then the interview with Tim Darwin is merely a follow-up to build a stronger case against King and that is the first thing we will make absolutely clear to Darwin's legal rep. If Darwin happens to spill something in the process, even better."

"You're getting quite devious in your old age," Whitton said with a wry smile on her face.

"If you can't beat them, join them."

Smith and Whitton had barely got through the doors of the station when DI Smyth pounced on them.

"The CPS has decided we've got more than enough to charge King," he said.

"So now the hard part begins," Smith said.

He told the DI about what happened with Tim Darwin.

"And you think a formal interview is the way forward?" DI Smyth said when Smith had finished.

"What harm can it do?"

"That depends on his lawyer. We have one suspect in custody, so you do realise how it's going to look if we bring in another suspect at this stage."

"As far as Darwin and his legal representative are concerned, Darwin is merely helping us to build a stronger case against Robert King."

"I'm not too sure about this," DI Smyth said. "If this goes wrong it could all blow up in our faces and I for one do not relish the thought of an outright fiasco in my first week in charge."

"It won't go wrong, boss," Smith was adamant. "If it will put your mind at rest, you can head up the interview. You can direct it as you see fit. I'll just sit in for appearance's sake."

DI Smyth sighed. "Why don't I believe that? What time is Darwin due in?"

"He's going to let me know."

"You'd better fill me in on what we know about the man in the meantime then. You do realise I'm sticking my neck out here."

"That's how we operate around here, boss," Smith turned around and a huge grin appeared on his face. He managed to control it and turned back to the DI once more. "Let's get a couple of cups of coffee from the canteen and I'll brief you on what we know so far."

"What was that all about?" Bridge had arrived by the front desk. "That husband of yours looks like he's won the lotto."

"Boys," Whitton said. "It looks like Smyth is already one-nil down in the territorial pissing competition."

She told him about Tim Darwin.

"How does Smith do it?" Bridge said. "He can get anyone to agree with him once he's set his mind to it."

"He's impossible to argue with," Whitton said. "It's as simple as that."

"I assume we're talking about Smith," Chalmers had come inside from a cigarette break.

"Who else?" Whitton said. "Robert King has been charged with the four murders."

"I heard. The evidence is pretty damning. The man had motive, opportunity and the capability to carry out the shootings. It sounds open and closed to me."
"Smith's not convinced, sir," Bridge told him.
"I'd be concerned if he was," Chalmers said.
"Smith and the DI are going to interview another suspect," Bridge added.
"I assume they're not interviewing this suspect as a *suspect*?"
"Precisely, sir."
"Good. Then it shouldn't go tits-up then. I'd better get going. I've got a meeting with the Super and the ACC. Old Smyth has been like a bear with sore head since his nephew arrived. I thought he'd be pleased."
"Just don't mention anything about a nine-iron golf club," Whitton told him.
"Chalmers frowned and walked off down the corridor shaking his head.

Half an hour later, Smith received a phone call from Tim Darwin. Darwin had informed him that he would be arriving at the station with his lawyer at two that afternoon. DI Smyth decided to call an emergency briefing before then to go over everything they had so far.
"You're all aware that Robert King has been charged with the murders of Charles Lincoln, Diana Wells, Wendy Price and Liam Lovelake," the DI began. "The CPS has ruled that the evidence against Mr King is more than enough." He paused for a moment.
"But," he continued. "You all know that this evidence alone isn't enough."
"With respect, sir," Bridge said. "The man is one of very few people who could have carried out shots like those – a woman he despised was one of the victims, and the murder weapon was found in his possession. I'd say that's enough."
"No, it's not." It was Smith. "I will only be satisfied when I hear King tell us he killed those four people."

"He's still denying it," Bridge said. "The DI and me had another crack at him while you were at the gun club and he's not budging. He's clearly lying."

"I still haven't made my mind up about that," Smith said.

Bridge was about to say something else when DI Smyth raised his hand to stop him.

"Right, if Robert King insists on denying any involvement in these shootings, let's look for something that can prove otherwise. What we have so far is this: Four victims – only one of whom is linked to Mr King in any way, and that is his ex-wife, Wendy. Her new husband has a watertight alibi in that he was away at a conference in London at the time, and this has been corroborated by a number of people. Diana Wells was the second victim. Pathology has confirmed she was pregnant when she died. Her husband, Gordon claims to have been at work at the time of the shooting. Mr Wells owns a specialised IT company and claims he was working alone in the office until after eleven that night. His personal login details prove he did in fact access the main system that night and therefore we can also rule him out.

The final victim was Liam Lovelake. Petty criminal and general all-round lowlife. Lovelake's friends and associates have all kept quiet, as I expected them to, but I do not believe any of them were involved anyway. And that leads me to my next point. Robert King has already told us of a plan hatched in Afghanistan to kill his wife and the way in which these murders have been carried out matches that plan exactly. As far as we are aware, only Mr King and Tim Darwin knew about this ingenious plot and Smith and I will be interviewing Darwin later this afternoon. He may be able to give us details of this plot that could implicate Robert King further. Does anybody have anything to add?"

"What about the first victim?" Yang Chu said. "Charles Lincoln? You haven't mentioned him."

"I do not believe he's important in the whole scheme of things. Mr Lincoln just happened to be in the wrong place at the wrong time. We've looked into his circumstances and there was nothing to suggest he was anything more than an unfortunate piece in a rather complicated puzzle. Anything else?"

"When you spoke to King earlier," Smith said. "Did you ask him if his alarm was armed?"

"Excuse me?"

"When we went inside his house, the alarm almost deafened us," Smith elaborated. "If King *was* set up, how did the real killer get past that alarm when he went in to plant the rifle? We need to find out if King armed it."

"All in good time," DI Smyth looked at his watch.

Smith knew from experience that was usually a clear indication that the briefing was about to end.

"I think we've gone over everything we can for now."

DI Smyth's words told Smith he hadn't been wrong.

CHAPTER FORTY ONE

"Interview with Timothy Darwin commenced, 14:05," DI Smyth began. "Present DS Smith and Mr Darwin's legal representative, Gregory Dean." The DI had decided that the interview with Tim Darwin should run concurrently with a follow-up interview with Robert King and Bridge and Whitton were in there with King now. Smith had asked Yang Chu to have a look at the ballistics and pathology reports to see if anything new jumped out at him.

"I assume the fact that my client is here voluntarily has been noted?" Dean spoke first.

"Smith pointed to the recording device. "It has now. Can we get started?"

"Mr Darwin," DI Smyth began. "Do you understand why you're here?"

"To put an end to this ridiculous farce," Tim said. "And I do have things to do so can we please get this over with as quickly as possible?"

"Of course. For the record, we have already spoken with Mr Darwin a number of times before. What we are here to ascertain today is Mr Darwin's thoughts on something that happened while he toured in Afghanistan. Could you please tell us when you were stationed in Afghanistan, Mr Darwin?"

"I was there from 2005 until the spring of 2006."

"And what was your role there?"

"I served as a Private affiliated to ISAF."

"That's the International Security Assistance Force?"

"That's correct."

"What were your duties within ISAF?" Smith asked him.

"After my basic training they found I had a talent for shooting, so I trained as a sniper."

"And what did that entail?" Smith said.

"Where is this line of questioning leading?" Gregory Dean asked.

"I'm merely forming an understanding of what your client did in Afghanistan."

"Please answer the question," DI Smyth said.

"To be honest," Darwin said. "Not much happened most of the time. We'd spend the days training and nights I'd read or write letters home. Then we got word from McNeill that we were to take back Musa Qala. The Taliban had taken the main town and McNeill decided it was imperative we take it back."

"Forgive me," Smith said. "But who is McNeill?"

"General McNeill was the American General in charge of ISAF," Darwin said in a tone that indicated Smith had asked a stupid question.

"Thank you," Smith said. "Go on."

"We were supposed to wait until dawn, but McNeill decided on a change of plan at the last minute. He reckoned the element of surprise would work."

"And did it?"

"No," Darwin sighed. "No, it didn't. It was obvious someone had tipped them off and they were waiting. We reached the ridge overlooking the town and immediately came under heavy fire. Rob and I got ready and took cover on either side of the RG and started picking off the enemy. There were too many of them and I ended up getting shot."

"Could you please run through the series of events that led up to you getting shot?" DI Smyth said.

"I told you all this earlier."

"For the record."

"There was a Taliban sniper dressed all in black," Darwin said. "I spotted him too late, and he shot me. It was as simple as that."

"Only it wasn't that simple was it?" Smith said. "You explained to us earlier that you were convinced Private Robert King had seen the enemy sniper and you believed King waited for him to shoot you before he took him down."

"I thought that at the time," Darwin said. "But afterwards when I'd had a chance to think, I knew Rob wouldn't have done that."

"I will ask you again, detectives," Gregory Dean said. "Where exactly are you going with this?"

"Please just bear with us," Smith said. "Mr Darwin, was this gunshot the reason you served such a short time in Afghanistan?"

"That's right. I was discharged soon after and I never went back. Could I get something to drink?"

"Interview with Timothy Darwin recommenced, 14:30," DI Smyth said. Darwin was now halfway through his second bottle of water.

"Mr Darwin, are you aware that Robert King has been charged with the murders of four people?"

"Of course – it's been all over the news."

"Do you believe Mr King to be capable of such killing?"

"No," Darwin replied without hesitating. "No, I don't. Rob killed people during a war – he would never shoot innocent people."

"OK," Smith said. "Let's talk about something else. Just before you were discharged from the army, Robert King told you about a plan he'd hatched up, didn't he?"

"I don't remember any plan."

"Let me elaborate. This ingenious plot involved killing his wife in such a way that there was no way the shadow of suspicion would fall on King. Does that ring any bells?"

"Oh that." The penny had dropped. "That was just a stupid fantasy Rob had dreamed up. He would never have carried it out in real life."

"For the record, Mr Darwin," DI Smyth said. "Could you outline Mr King's plan?"

"If I remember it was something about sending you lot in the wrong direction from the very beginning. There is one victim – one person you want to kill, but you kill the others to make it look like a string of murders. And you don't kill the main target first. That way the police will start by looking for a link to the victims and totally miss the fact that only one of them was the main target."

"Does that plan sound familiar?" Smith said. "You've just said it's been all over the news."

"Are you telling me that Rob has actually carried out his plan?"

"It seems that way, unless there is somebody else who knew about it."

"But Rob and I were alone on the range that morning. What exactly are you trying to say?"

"Yes, detective," Gregory Dean spoke. "What is it you're implying here? Is my client a suspect now?"

"Not at all," DI Smyth said. "As far as we know, Mr King came up with a plan for a complicated murder – one that he knew would be unlikely to lead back to himself. Now, someone has put that plan into action. Are there any other details of Rob's plan you can remember?"

"I really didn't pay much attention to it. Like I told you I assumed it was just some way for Rob to deal with his wife running off with another man. It wasn't something he was planning on acting on."

 "I think this interview has run its course," Gregory Dean said. "If my client is not a suspect then you are aware he is free to leave at any time."

"Of course," Smith said. "There's just one thing. When we spoke to your client earlier, he refused to cooperate when we asked about his whereabouts on certain days. I'm sure you'll agree with me that it would be in his best interests if he gave us some answers?"

He took out a piece of paper and placed it on the table in front of Tim Darwin. "The dates and times are all there. We already know you were home alone for the first one. What about the other three?"

Darwin glanced at the piece of paper. "I went out with my wife on Friday evening – her mother was looking after Ryan, our son and our teenage daughter was staying with a friend, so we took advantage and went to this new Indian restaurant in town. We got back just after ten. My wife will be able to confirm this. Sunday afternoon we fetched Ryan from his Nan's house at four. We stayed there a couple of hours, so there will be two people to corroborate my story, and Monday I was out in Rievaulx taking photos of the Abbey. All my photos are time stamped."

"Why didn't you tell us all this before?" DI Smyth said. "Why didn't you tell us you had alibis for the times three of the shootings took place? You could have saved us all a lot of time and effort."

"Not to mention legal bills," Smith glanced over at Gregory Dean. "Judging by that suit, I doubt he comes cheap."

CHAPTER FORTY TWO

"Robert King isn't budging," Bridge came into the canteen with Whitton and sat next to Smith. "He's sticking to his story."

"Tim Darwin has alibis for three of the shootings," Smith said. "We still need to check them, but I've got a feeling he's telling the truth."

"What I don't understand," Whitton joined in. "Is why didn't he just tell us where he was when we asked him this morning? Why drag it out like this?"

"It doesn't matter," Smith said. "What matters is we're back to square one."

"We've still got King," Bridge said.

"He'll go before a jury and they'll probably convict," Smith sighed. "The evidence against him is pretty damning but I still need to hear it from him. Did you ask him about his alarm system?"

"He reckons he never leaves the house without arming it. It would have gone off if someone had broken in."

"OK," Smith rubbed his temples. "The freezer the rifle was found in hadn't been used for quite some time. If King was framed, we can assume the rifle was placed inside the freezer after the last shooting. So, sometime between Monday morning and yesterday afternoon, somebody broke into Rob King's house, somehow managed to get past the alarm system and hid the Arctic L96 inside Rob King's meat freezer."

"That's if King was actually framed," Bridge said. "We're spending all this time and effort speculating – maybe for once you should just accept the fact that the feeling in your gut is wrong and we have the murderer safely locked up in the cells downstairs."

"I'll accept it when I'm convinced."

He stood up and immediately felt a throbbing pain in his head. He walked over to the window and closed his eyes.

"Are you alright?" It was Whitton. "Can you feel another migraine coming on?"

"I'll be alright." Smith took the two pills from his pocket, unwrapped them and popped them both in his mouth. "Are we positive that Tim Darwin was the only other person who knew about Robert King's plan to kill his wife? Maybe King told someone else about it."

"He reckons he didn't," Whitton said. "We asked him about it again and he said Darwin and he were alone on the range that day. King's spotter had gone to the toilet. Are you sure you're alright? You look a bit pale."

"It'll pass when these tablets kick in."

Smith stared out of the window at the spires of the Minster in the distance. The pain over his left eye was subsiding – the pills seemed to be doing the trick. He desperately wanted Robert King to be their killer – it would be so much simpler if that was the case, but Smith couldn't shrug off the feeling that it wasn't King.

He returned to the table. "We need to check out Robert King's military records."

"What the hell for?" Bridge didn't hold back.

"Because we haven't had a look at them, and we should have done."

"And what exactly are you hoping to achieve from finding out what someone did in the army ten years ago?"

"I don't know yet. Do you have any better ideas?"

"Actually, I do," Bridge stood up and looked Smith directly in the eye. "My idea would be to stop wasting unnecessary time and effort on a wild goose chase and let the legal system decide if the man we've arrested is guilty of these shootings or not. That would be my idea."

Smith took a step closer to him and a feeling of déjà vu washed over him. It seemed as if he and Bridge had had this exact moment not so long ago. Smith remembered how that one had ended – he'd punched Bridge so hard he'd almost knocked him unconscious. He stepped back a few paces. Whitton was already on her feet.

"That's enough, you two. Bridge, go and see if you can find something to do. Smith, are you trying to induce another migraine? Take a break, Go outside and smoke a cigarette. Both of you please stop bickering. It's driving me insane."

Smith and Bridge looked at one another. Even though, technically they both held a higher rank than Whitton, neither of them dared to refuse her orders. They set off down the stairs and both of them headed outside. Smith lit a cigarette. After a couple of drags the tension in his head eased off slightly.

"I wouldn't like to get on the wrong side of Whitton when she's really angry," Bridge said.

Smith laughed and coughed out the smoke he'd been holding inside. He coughed a few more times and wiped his eyes.

"Sorry about that," Bridge said.

"Next time wait until I don't have a mouth full of smoke," Smith said and coughed once more.

"I wasn't talking about the coughing fit. I mean sorry for doubting your judgment. I ought to know better by now."

"I'm not at all sure what's happening here, but I sure as hell get the feeling that Rob King doesn't fit somehow. It just feels wrong."

"What does the DI think?"

"He's also not sure. What do you think of him so far?"

"I've been pleasantly surprised. But he seems to like you so he must be a shit judge of character."

"Cheeky bastard. I'm starting to warm to him, and he listens and I never would have expected that from an ex-army bloke."

"Do you really think we'll find anything from sifting through King's old army records?"

"What harm can it do? I know you think we've got him, but I've got this nasty habit of wanting to know why. If we're right in thinking King's plan was carried out, then we've got three totally innocent victims here."

"And we've got some sick bastard out there who doesn't care," Bridge added.

CHAPTER FORTY THREE

Smith stubbed out his cigarette and headed back inside the station. Bridge said he needed to make a phone call, so Smith left him outside. Superintendent Jeremy Smyth and his nephew were talking next to the wall to the side of the front desk. From their body language and the tone of their voices it was clear the conversation was not a hostile one. Baldwin was talking on the phone behind the front desk. She replaced the handset and sighed.

"Problems?" Smith asked her.

"That person really has problems," she told him. "Can you believe a man just phoned and asked us if we can help find his rabbit?"

"You're kidding?"

"I wish I was. His rabbit got through the fence at the back of his garden and escaped into the allotments at the back and he asked if we could organise a search of the allotments."

"What did you tell him?" Smith was finding it hard not to laugh.

"I told him the bunny would probably come back when it was ready."

"What did he say to that?"

"He said that's what the rabbit normally did," Baldwin said. "Can you believe it? He then told me the stupid rabbit has been hitting the road on a regular basis for months, but it always comes back. That's exactly why I joined the police – to listen to nonsense like that."

"I've got a job for you," Smith told her. "And it doesn't involve locating missing bunnies."

"Thank God."

"I need you to get hold of Robert King's army records. I'm not sure what they're going to tell us, but I can't just sit back and do nothing."

"I'll get onto it."

"Thanks, Baldwin, and if the rabbit man phones back tell him I'll be more than willing to help."

"Are you kidding me?"

"Tell him I've got a rather large Bull Terrier who would love the opportunity to chase a rabbit around the allotments."

Baldwin laughed. "I'll let you know what I come up with."

DI Smyth was still chatting to the Superintendent when Smith walked past. He walked past them and headed for his office but was stopped in his tracks.

"Ah, Smith."

Smith groaned inwardly and turned around.

"Smith," the Superintendent said again. "Oliver has just been filling me in on the good news. I knew it was a good move to bring another Smyth into the midst. If I had my way I'd fill all the strategic positions with Smyth's.

God help us all, Smith thought.

"What was it?" Smyth hadn't quite finished yet. "Three days?"

"Four, sir," his nephew corrected him. "It was four days between the first shooting and us arresting Robert King."

"That's simply outstanding. Outstanding, and all because a Smyth stepped in and took control."

"To be honest, sir," DI Smyth said. "I had very limited input in this one. I've still been finding my feet, and it was actually a team effort that brought this investigation to its swift conclusion."

"Nonsense. A team is only as good as the man at the helm allows them to be."

Smith and DI Smyth both glanced at each other. Both of them seemed equally confused by the Superintendent's last sentence.

"I'd better get back to work," Smith said. "I've got a lot of paperwork to catch up on."

"That can wait. We have more important matters to discuss. I believe we've been seen in a much more favourable light by the general public recently, and as such I am keen to keep that momentum going."

Smith knew exactly what was coming next.

Two words he dreaded more than any others.

"It is imperative that we arrange a press conference as soon as possible."

Press conference.

"I'll leave you to it then," Smith said.

"I was hoping you would lead," Smyth said, and Smith knew he wasn't asking.

He thought hard for a second. A press conference was the last thing he wanted right now, especially when he wasn't one-hundred percent certain the man they had in custody was actually guilty.

"With respect, sir," Smith said it with as much sincerity as he could muster. "Don't you agree this would be the ideal opportunity to introduce the people of York to the new DI?"

He purposefully avoided looking at DI Smyth as he spoke.

"I don't know," the DI said.

"No," his uncle looked especially pleased. "DS Smith is right. It's a splendid idea. I'll introduce you to our liaison officer personally."

Smith still couldn't bring himself to look at DI Smyth. He headed off in the direction of his office, all the time he could feeling the DI's eyes burning into the back of his head.

Smith sat in front of his computer, but he didn't switch it on. He leaned back in his chair and rubbed the back of his neck. He was sure there were knots there that hadn't been there a few weeks ago – tight knots that wouldn't disappear no matter how hard he kneaded them. He closed his eyes and breathed in deeply. The pain in his head had gone – the tablets had obviously worked.

Smith was woken by a hand on his shoulder. He shook his head and turned around. Baldwin was standing behind him.

"Sorry," he said. "I must have dozed off. What time is it?"

"It's almost five. I emailed you those army records you asked for – I'm about to knock off for the day but I wasn't sure if you received them."

"I didn't switch my PC on," Smith said. "I think I'll head home myself. Thanks, Baldwin."

He turned on his PC and when it had booted up, he opened up his email and checked to see if the army records were there. They were. There were a large number of attachments with the email. Smith didn't bother to open up the mail – he forwarded the whole lot to his home email address, waited for them to send and then he shut down his computer.

CHAPTER FORTY FOUR

Smith stopped at a supermarket on the way home and bought some groceries. His fridge was almost empty, and the dogs had run out of food. It had also been so long since he'd cooked a proper meal and he wasn't sure what he had in his freezer. After loading his car with more than ten shopping bags he set off home. He could hear the dogs barking before he'd even reached the front door and wondered what was making them so excited. He was sure the barking was coming from inside the house. He thought back to that morning and was sure he'd let them out the back door. He left the shopping in the car and opened his front door. Fred, the hideous Pug was on him in a flash with Theakston, the Bull Terrier not far behind.

"Easy, boys," Smith said. "How did you get inside the house? Did I forget to let you out?"

"I let them in."

Whitton appeared in the hallway.

Smith was confused. "What are you doing here? Where's your car? Where's Laura? Is she here with you?"

"Can you at least close the front door before you start interrogating me?"

"Sorry," Smith closed the door. "Where were we?"

"You were giving me the Spanish inquisition," Whitton said. "Where have you been? Baldwin said you left the station over an hour ago."

"I was running low on supplies, and speaking of which, my car boot is full of shopping. Do you want to give me a hand offloading them? Then you can answer my questions."

Twenty minutes later the shopping had been packed away. Smith opened the back door and he and Whitton went outside with the dogs close behind.

"Well?" Smith lit a cigarette and sat on the wooden bench.

"I've forgotten the questions," Whitton said.

"I think I asked what you were doing here first."

"I want to try," Whitton sat opposite him. "For Laura's sake and for ours."

"Where is Laura?"

"She fell asleep in the car on the way from my parents' house, so I've put her upstairs in your bed."

"Our bed," Smith reminded her. "Where's your car?"

"In the garage where it always goes."

"Wasn't that a bit presumptuous? How did you know I wouldn't send you packing?"

"Moron."

"Sorry," Smith said. "What exactly does this mean?"

"It's a start, and we'll see from there. I had a chat with my dad, and he suggested we give it a go. I'll sleep in the spare bed."

"Of course," Smith realised he was beaming from ear to ear. "I told you – your terms, and I promise I won't pressure you into anything. You'll be ready when you're ready. Are you hungry?"

"I am actually," and if I know that daughter of ours, she's going to be begging like a dog as soon as she smells whatever you're going to cook us."

Whitton wasn't exaggerating. Smith rustled up some frozen lasagne and salad and Laura's voice could be heard upstairs before the oven had even preheated. Smith was up the stairs in a flash and he returned shortly afterwards with a hungry four-year-old in tow.

"It's still got another half an hour," he told her and peeled a banana for her to eat in the meantime.

She toddled out to the back garden to see if anything had changed in her absence.

"This is nice," Smith said while he chopped the salad. "I never thought I'd ever get this back again.

"Did you buy beer on your shopping exhibition?" Whitton asked.

"I've always got beer. Get me one too. You know where it is."

"Don't push it."

Smith finished making the salad and they went outside to the garden while they waited for the lasagne to cook. Laura was chasing the dogs at the bottom by the fence.

"What have you been feeding her?" Smith asked Whitton. "She gets bigger every time I see her."

"She loves my mum's cooking. How's the headache?"

"Gone. Those tablets the doctor gave me really seem to work."

"Well make sure you always carry some around with you."

"I think I might have upset the DI," Smith said and finished what was left in his bottle.

"Already? How did you do that?"

"The Super wanted me to head up an urgent press conference and I suggested the DI do it instead. Smyth thought it was a great idea. I think the word, *splendid* was used. The DI was far from pleased."

"I suppose it is a good idea, though," Whitton said. "It'll introduce the press to the new DI and give the Super a bit of an ego boost at the same time."

"There was another reason I didn't want to do the press conference," Smith turned serious. "I still don't think Robert King is our man. All the evidence points to him, but something is still not right."

The alarm on the oven sounded to let them know the lasagne was cooked.

"Saved by the bell," Whitton stood up. "No more work talk tonight, alright?"

"I was planning to have a look at something Baldwin sent over," Smith said. "I asked her to get hold of Robert King's army records."

"What do you actually expect to find from some old army records?"

"I have no idea. Let's go and eat. And I promise no more work talk until that lasagne is finished."

CHAPTER FORTY FIVE

"I don't think I could eat another thing," Smith placed his knife and fork on his plate. "That wasn't bad at all. And Laura seemed to enjoy it."
"No more frozen meals for a while though. We need to start eating healthier."
"I'll run Laura a bath," Smith offered. "I've missed it."
He headed upstairs.

Smith turned on the taps and tested the water. He wasn't quite sure how he felt. He wasn't expecting to come home and discover that some semblance of his previous life had returned. However it was going to turn out he was determined that he was going to do everything he could to make sure he didn't lose his wife and daughter again. He didn't care that Whitton would be sleeping in the spare room - at least she would be in the same house. They would drink coffee together in the morning and she would be the last person he would see at night. It was much more than he ever expected.
"The bath's ready," he shouted down the stairs.

Laura's eyes started to droop before Smith had even dried her. He let Whitton dry her hair and dress her in her pyjamas and they both went to the spare room to lay her down to bed.
"I think it'll be better if she wakes up with me there," Whitton said. "For the first few nights back anyway."
"She kicks in her sleep, you know," Smith said. "She's got a hell of a left foot."
"Nice try. I'm going back downstairs. She's lights' out already."
"I want to stay here for a bit," Smith said. "I just want to look at her. For a while."

Whitton kissed him on the top of the head and left the room. Smith leaned over and carefully did the same to their daughter. He breathed in deeply and took in her scent. He did this once more then went downstairs to join Whitton.

He found her outside in the garden. "I wish I could nod off so easily – she must get that from you."

"I've never had any trouble sleeping," Whitton said. "It's all to do with having a clear conscience."

"I've normally got a clear conscience," Smith protested. "Most of the time I can't sleep when a case is bugging me."

"Like this one for example?"

"I told you – something doesn't feel right about Robert King. How many killers have we come across over the years?"

"I've lost count."

"Does King strike you as a cold-blooded murderer?"

"He was a sniper in Afghanistan," she reminded him. "He killed God knows how many people over there."

"There was a war going on, and it was his job. I just can't see him as somebody who could kill three people he doesn't even know just so he can get away with killing his ex-wife. It's too far-fetched."

"I'm not going to stop you talking about work, am I?"

"You know you're not."

"Then we might as well grab a couple more beers."

"I want to have a look at King's army records. There's something in there that we haven't thought of yet."

"Why don't you get a more modern PC?" Whitton said after Smith's old computer still hadn't warmed up after five minutes.

"I like this one. It's like an old car – it takes a while to get going but once it's up and running you can't kill it. Here we go."

He typed in his password and opened up his email. The mail he'd sent himself was the last one on there. He opened up the first attachment.

"This is a lot of information," Whitton looked at all the attachments that arrived with the email. "How did Baldwin get hold of all this?"

"I don't ask," Smith said. "She has her sources. This looks like his basic training evaluation."

He scrolled down the page and read the document.

"According to this he scored very highly on the physical side of things," Smith said. "But he was far from an academic. He completed his basic training in Pirbright in the summer of 2005. There's not much else on here."

He opened the next attachment. In it were details of Robert King's medical history.

"He suffered a short bout of flu while he was completing his advanced individual training, but besides that he stayed relatively healthy. He completed his AIT in the autumn of 2005 and was sent to Afghanistan almost immediately afterwards."

"Isn't that unusual?" Whitton asked. "To be sent to the front line straight after training?"

"I don't think so. That's what the training is for."

The next few attachments detailed King's time in Afghanistan.

"He was posted in Afghanistan just in time for the winter," Smith continued. "After a brief basic training module in adverse weather warfare, he was based in Helmand Province at a place called Camp Bastion."

"I've heard my dad mention it a few times," Whitton said. "I think it was the main military hub in that area."

"And," Smith carried on. "According to these files, nothing much happened there. Here are some details of some of the shooting competitions he competed in. He really was very good. He only lost one competition in all the time he was there."

"How long was he at Camp Bastion?"

Smith scrolled down once more. "Eighteen months. He saw a bit of action in and around the camp, but it was at Musa Qala in early 2006 that things really got going."

"That was where Tim Darwin got shot," Whitton remembered.

"Exactly. And after that, besides a few minor skirmishes with the Taliban, there wasn't much more action. It appears the Americans took over and the British contingency of ISAF was reduced to almost nothing in the years that followed. I'm going outside for a smoke."

"Are you satisfied now?" Whitton asked him outside. "Are you satisfied that Robert King's army records have no bearing whatsoever on what has happened here over the past week?"

"Not yet." Smith lit a cigarette. "There has to be something there – we've only covered half the material."

"I'm going to bed," Whitton said. "I don't think my brain can process any more information. I'll see you in the morning."

"I'm going to stay up for a while," Smith said.

"I know you are."

"I'll find something – you mark my words."

"Good night," Whitton moved closer and hugged him.

"Thank you," was all Smith could think of to say.

Whitton smiled and went back inside.

CHAPTER FORTY SIX

Whitton came into the kitchen to find the back door open. She glanced at the clock on the microwave and saw it was still very early. She'd spent the night being kicked and manhandled by a four-year-old and when the sun began to shine through the window in the spare room, she'd conceded defeat.

She found Smith outside. He was slumped over the wooden bench with an unlit cigarette in his hand. Whitton rubbed the back of his neck and he stirred.
"Have you been out here all night?" she asked him.
He opened his eyes. "What time is it?"
"Just after seven. What are you doing out here?"
"I came out for a smoke, and I must have fallen asleep."
A smile appeared on his face.
"You found something didn't you?"
"I think so," the smile was still plastered all over Smith's face.
"What?"
"I'm not sure yet. I need to make a few phone calls when we get to work, but I think it's something important."
"Come on," Whitton said. "What did you find?"
"Let's just say that someone in this investigation hasn't been completely honest with us."

* * *

An hour later they both walked inside the station. They'd dropped Laura off at day-care on the way. Bridge and Yang Chu came in a short time later. Bridge was beaming from ear to ear.
"What's wrong with you?" Smith asked him. "New girlfriend?"
"That's not all I care about you know," Bridge said.

"Since when?" Smith countered.

"I'm much deeper than that."

"What's with the grin then?"

"I just happened to notice that you and Whitton arrived in the same car," Bridge told him. "It looks like things are improving for you."

"I need to make a few phone calls in my office," Smith said. "There have been a few developments and I just need to make absolutely sure of a few things. When DI Smyth arrives tell him we need to have an emergency briefing. Let's say in an hour."

"What's going on with Smith this morning?" Bridge asked Whitton in the canteen. "Why's he being so cryptic?"

"He wouldn't tell me," Whitton replied. "But I think he's found something important. I left him poring over Robert King's army records last night and I found him asleep in the garden this morning."

"I wonder what it is he's found."

"Did you see the press conference last night?" Yang Chu said.

"I missed it," Whitton said. "Anything exciting happen?"

"You could say that. The Super really outdid himself in the stupidity stakes this time."

"What did he do?" Bridge asked. "I missed it too."

"Let's just say he got eaten alive," Yang Chu said. "There was this one journo from one of the big dailies who seemed to take a dislike to old Smyth, and he cut him down with everything the Super said. Luckily the DI came to the rescue and shut down the whole thing pretty sharpish. I'll be surprised if the Super shows his face today."

DI Smyth came in. He looked absolutely exhausted. He got some coffee from the machine in the corner and sat down at their table.

"Smith's found something," Whitton informed him. "Something in Robert King's army records. He wanted me to tell you we need to hold an emergency briefing to go over whatever it is he found."

"Well I hope it's something positive," the DI said. "We need to try and get back some respect for the police after my uncle did his utmost to make us look like incompetents last night."

"What did he do?" Whitton asked.

"Some hack obviously has it in for him and he made him look like an imbecile."

"With respect..." Bridge started.

"I know," DI Smyth said. "I know he is an imbecile, but he really went to town last night. I wouldn't be surprised if Robert King's defense lawyer uses a transcript of the press conference at the trial."

"Here you all are," Smith came in. "Seeing as we're all here, we might as well have the briefing in here."

"What have you found?" DI Smyth asked him.

Smith got some coffee and sat down. "I spent the whole night looking over Robert King's army records. At first, nothing much jumped out at me, but when I read them again, I spotted something. Robert King represented the army as a marksman. And looking through the competition records it's clear he was very good at it. In over ten competitions he only lost once."

"Where are we going with this?" Bridge asked. "We already know he's a hotshot deadeye."

"What I didn't know," Smith carried on. "Is that each deadeye has a spotter. A right-hand-man if you like. I looked it up on the net, and these spotters are usually keen marksmen themselves but they're not quite good enough to actually shoot. The competition results list the deadeye and the spotter and Robert King's spotter was a man by the name of Welly. Then I remembered something Tim Darwin said. There was a photograph on his wall taken after one of the competitions. Darwin was in the photo, as was Robert King. King's spotter was also on the photo. Welly. Something about that name made me think, so I went through the list of the people who were in King's squadron and there was no mention of anyone by the name of Welly. In fact, there was nobody with a name remotely like Welly. I managed to get the contact details of a man who was also there at the same time as King – a Corporal George Peters. He's since left the army, but he told me something interesting. Welly wasn't part of King's squadron – that's why I couldn't find his name on the personnel list, he was there in an admin role. IT as it happens. And the nickname Welly is because his surname is Wells. Welly is Gordon Wells, the husband of the second victim."

CHAPTER FORTY SEVEN

"What does it actually mean though?" Bridge asked.

"It means Gordon Wells lied to us," Smith said.

"Not really. All it means is he didn't mention the fact that he served in Afghanistan. Why would he? It still doesn't mean he was involved in all this."

"I haven't finished yet," Smith said. "Corporal Peters was very talkative, and something happened to Gordon Wells that resulted in his swift departure from the army."

"What happened?" DI Smyth asked.

"It was after a competition," Smith said. "Apparently the whole barracks were there. King was up against his biggest rival and it ended in the last round before a sudden death shoot-out. According to Peters, King and this rival were neck and neck and King needed a perfect ten to tie. The wind had picked up, but King hadn't noticed it. His spotter didn't notice it either. Anyway, King took the shot, missed the centre and only then realised the wind had changed. Corporal Peters reckons he was furious. And he blamed Gordon Wells for the whole thing."

"What has this got to do with the recent shootings?" Bridge said. "I still can't see where you're going with this."

"Just hear me out. Corporal Peters told me that something happened in the barracks later that night. Gordon Wells woke the whole camp up with his screaming. He jumped out of bed and when someone checked they found a yellow scorpion inside. That is a very nasty scorpion. It stung Wells on the inside of his leg. Corporal Peters reckons everybody knew where the scorpion came from."

"Robert King?" Yang Chu suggested.

"Right. Peters told me that King was always showing off picking up scorpions and proving how brave he was. It's quite obvious he put the scorpion in

Wells' bed to pay him back for losing the competition. Wells had a particularly bad reaction to the sting and was hospitalised for three weeks. He was sent home shortly afterwards."

Bridge stood up and went to get some more coffee from the machine. "I still can't see what this has to do with the shootings," he said. "Gordon Wells was a spotter, not a deadeye. He would have never been able to make any of the shots that killed those four people."

"That's what I thought too," Smith said. "There were two top snipers at the time – Robert King and Tim Darwin. Both Privates. Gordon Wells was also a Private but his role there was far away from any action so most people assumed he was just some pen-pusher, but according to one of the women he worked with, Wells could shoot."

"OK," DI Smyth said. "This is all well and good, but what have we actually got here? A man whose wife was the second victim. A man who served in Afghanistan with our main suspect. What does that actually prove?"

"Wells was hospitalised because of Robert King," Smith said. "He was discharged from the army because of what King did. We need to speak to Gordon Wells again. I want to find out why he didn't mention all this before."

"I hate to be a downer," Bridge said. "But I think you're barking up the wrong tree here. Clutching at straws. I can't see how anything of what you've just told us can have any relevance to the investigation. I think it's time you faced facts and admitted you were wrong for once. The man we have in custody is our deadeye. It's as simple as that."

Smith looked around the table. It was quite clear from the expressions on the faces of the people sitting there that they shared Bridge's views.

Smith looked from face to face.

"Whitton, surely you must admit it's odd that Wells didn't mention he'd been in Afghanistan with King."

"I'm sorry," she said. "But I agree with Bridge. Why would he? And what would he possibly have to gain by killing his wife? She was pregnant, remember? He was looking forward to being a father."

"I need to go and speak to him," Smith wasn't giving up.

"Stop this right now," DI Smyth had raised his voice. "This is nonsense. And we've got better things to do than waste our time on dead-ends like this."

"I'm going outside for a smoke."

Smith glared at DI Smyth, stood up and left the canteen.

* * *

The offices of Wells IT were situated in a newly built office park two streets up from the river. Wells IT occupied the whole of the top floor. Smith got out of the lift and followed the directions Gordon Wells' secretary had given him to Wells' office. The door was open. Smith knocked and went inside.

"Good morning," Wells stood up. "Can I get you something to drink? Coffee? Tea?"

"No thanks," Smith said. "I need to ask you a few questions."

"Take a seat. What's this about? I've got a lot of work to get through today."

"Why didn't you tell me you knew Robert King?" Smith came straight to the point.

"You didn't ask."

"And you didn't think to mention the fact that you were a spotter in Afghanistan? Your wife was killed by a sniper, Mr Wells, and I find it very odd that you didn't tell us what you did at Camp Bastion."

"I've put that life behind me, detective," Wells said rather gruffly. "And if you've come here merely to remind me of it then I suggest you leave right now."

"I'm not finished yet. What is your opinion of Private Robert King?"

"Private King was an arrogant man," Wells said. "Arrogant with a nasty streak a mile long and I'll tell you now that's a dangerous combination."
"I believe Private King was the reason for your discharge from the army?"
"I couldn't prove it," Wells said. "But, yes, I believe he was."
"You must have been pretty angry about that. I know I would have been."
"What is this all about? Am I being accused of something here? Because that's what it sounds like to me. In case you've forgotten, I've recently lost my wife and unborn baby, and I do not appreciate you coming to my place of work and speaking to me like this."
"Do you still shoot, Mr Wells? I believe you used to be quite a marksman in your day."
"I think it's time you left," Wells said. "Or must I call security?"
"This isn't over," Smith said and walked out of the office.

CHAPTER FORTY EIGHT

Smith didn't feel like going back to work. He didn't know what he was going to do. He felt isolated. He'd never experienced the isolation he now felt within the team before. None of them had taken him seriously. Not even his wife.

Maybe I am losing my touch, he thought. *Maybe the time has come to do something else.*

The more he thought about it the more he realised how ridiculous his suspicions about Gordon Wells actually were. The only motive Wells had for killing all of those people and framing Robert King for it was his hatred of King. And if all he wanted to achieve was to send King to jail for something he hadn't done, surely he wouldn't kill his own wife in the process, especially knowing she was carrying his child.

Smith got inside his car and closed the door. He closed his eyes and went through everything that had happened in the past week in his head. Charles Lincoln had been killed in a crowded park early in the morning. Diana Wells was next – she was shot that night inside her apartment. Robert King's ex-wife was the third victim. Shot outside a supermarket during the day. Then Liam Lovelake. Robert King had come up with a plan to kill his cheating wife. The plan was identical to the recent sniper shootings.

One target but four victims.

The only person other than King who knew about the plot was Tim Darwin. Darwin had been on the range that day with King. There was nobody else around.

"Welly," Smith said out loud. "Gordon Wells was there that day."

Tim Darwin had told them that Welly had gone to the toilet. But what if he'd come back without them realising? What if he'd heard Robert King tell Tim Darwin his ingenious plot?"

Smith knew that *what-ifs* were not going to get him anywhere. His mobile phone started to ring. He looked at the screen and saw it was Whitton. He let it go to voicemail. A few seconds later the phone beeped to tell him he'd received a voice message and then a different sound informed him a text had been sent. He opened it up. It was from Whitton.
Gordon Wells has laid a formal complaint against you. You need to sort this out, Jason. I'm worried about you.
Smith read the message again. He put the phone back in his pocket and turned the key in the ignition.

* * *

Theakston and Fred wouldn't stop barking. Both dogs knew Smith was inside the house but he hadn't bothered to let them in. He turned on his PC and made some coffee while he waited for it to warm up. He took the coffee to the living room and opened up Robert King's army records once more. The coffee had gone cold by the time he'd finished reading through the attachments. He scrolled back up to King's medical history and learned once more that besides a brief bout of flu, King had been relatively healthy.
"What am I looking for?" he said out loud.
Then he thought of something. He took out his phone and dialled Baldwin's number.
She answered immediately. "Where are you? Everyone's looking for you."
"It doesn't matter where I am," Smith told her. "I need you to do something for me."
"I can't. You need to get back here right now."
"Please, Baldwin, I need you to get hold of the army medical records for Gordon Wells. He was discharged from service early 2006."
"I can't do that," Baldwin told him. "You know I can't do that."
"This is important, Baldwin," Smith said and realised he'd raised his voice. "Please. Send them to my home email."

He rang off and hoped that Baldwin would do what he'd asked.

While he waited to find out, Smith went outside and smoked a cigarette. The dogs seemed confused. The Portly Bull Terrier and the gruesome Pug sat at his feet and stared at him as though he'd grown another head. Smith finished the cigarette and went back inside to check his email. Baldwin had come through for him with Gordon Wells' army records. Smith's heart started to beat quickly as he read. Wells had been admitted to the hospital inside Camp Bastion in February 2006. He spent three weeks there and was discharged when he was deemed well enough to travel home. He'd suffered severe complications from the scorpion sting and at one stage these complications were life-threatening. The report was very detailed. Gordon Wells had sustained a yellow scorpion sting on the inside of his left leg. The effects of the venom had paralysed the leg and lower abdomen for forty-eight hours. The poison had made its way upwards in the direction of the heart and on its way there it had caused considerable damage to a number of organs. The pancreas had been affected as had parts of the liver and one kidney. Smith read further then stopped and read the section once more. Gordon Wells had suffered severe damage to the epididymis tubes inside the testes due to the close proximity of these to the sting site. The damage was irreversible, and the result was: Gordon Wells was unable to produce sperm. "Wells was infertile," Smith said out loud. "The baby his wife was carrying wasn't his."

CHAPTER FORTY NINE

"Where the hell have you been?" DI Smyth had been sitting behind his desk when Smith stormed in.

"Gordon Wells is our deadeye," Smith told him.

"Gordon Wells wants your blood. You really upset him by shouting the odds in his office and he's lodged a complaint against you."

"Fuck him. Let him try. He's our killer."

Smith told the DI what he'd found out about Wells.

"It still doesn't prove anything," DI Smyth said when Smith was finished. "So the baby wasn't his. It happens."

"It's him. He told me how he and his wife had been trying for years to conceive and how happy he was about it. He knew he couldn't have kids. He was there when Robert King told Tim Darwin about his plan for the perfect murder. King's ex wasn't the target – Diana Wells was, and Wells decided to kill two birds with one stone by framing the man who was responsible for making him infertile in the first place."

"Hold on," DI Smyth seemed to be taking Smith more seriously now. "What about the shooting itself – Wells is by no means a deadeye, so how do you explain that."

"The man is as good if not better than King," Smith said. "I did some digging and it turns out Wells has won competitions himself. The only difference between him and King is Wells keeps quiet about it."

"OK, how do you explain how he managed to get past King's alarm system and plant the rifle in King's kitchen?"

"I looked up the security company," Smith said. "*Stay Well Security*. Stay Well. Gordon Wells. It's his bloody company, boss – a side venture of his. He's got the access codes to all the alarms in the houses of the people who use his services."

"He had an alibi for the time his wife was killed," DI Smyth wasn't making it easy for Smith.

"I thought about that too," Smith said. "And we didn't ask him where he was when the other people were killed. Why would we? On the night Diana Wells was shot, he claimed to be at the office. The logins to the central system at the office proved he was there, but I checked that too. Wells' main business is automation. Remote access to systems, which means it would be quite possible to access the central system from anywhere providing you have the access codes and as the owner of the company, Gordon Wells most definitely has."

"Right," DI Smyth stood up. "We need to bring him in."

"He's not at the office anymore," Smith told him. "I checked. His secretary said he wasn't feeling very well, and he went home. I'm going to get there right away. I'll take Whitton with me."

"You will not go there alone. I want full back-up on this one."

"I'll get hold of Whitton in the meantime."

Smith found her by the front desk.

"Where have you been?" she said. "The DI wants your balls on a plate. Gordon Wells…"

"Is our deadeye," Smith interrupted her. "We need to bring him in right now. Let's go."

"What are you talking about? I thought…"

"I'll explain on the way," Smith cut her short again. "Wells left work, and I think he knows we're onto him. Come on."

Whitton's phone started to ring. She answered it and followed Smith outside to the car park.

"Get in," Smith opened up his car.

Whitton was still talking on the phone.

"Come on," Smith urged.

Whitton ended the call.

"That was Laura's day-care. I need to go and pick her up. They can't get hold of my parents and they say Laura has been throwing up. It sounds like she's really sick. I'll get Yang Chu to go with you."

She went back inside the station. Smith banged his hands on the dashboard. He kept his eyes on the door to the station.

"Fuck this," Smith said after a minute had passed and Yang Chu still hadn't appeared.

He turned the key in the ignition and sped out of the car park. He drove far too quickly in the direction of the river and screeched to a halt outside the apartment blocks where Gordon Wells lived. He looked up at the penthouses and thought about what he was going to do. He knew he needed to wait for backup, but he was afraid Wells would get away in the meantime.

Something flashed in his peripheral vision and the next moment the windscreen of his car exploded. Smith swept the broken glass from his face and inspected himself to see if he'd been injured. He couldn't find anything that would suggest he was hurt. He looked at the back windscreen and saw that the bullet had gone straight through. Whoever fired the shot had been aiming at the passenger side. His mobile phone started to ring.

"Whitton," he answered it without looking at the screen.

"You know what I'm capable of." It was Gordon Wells' voice. "So I suggest you bear that in mind."

"I'm coming for you, Wells," Smith said.

The phone went dead for a moment and then another bullet whizzed past Smith's head and shattered the back windscreen. Smith raised his hand to his ear and realised it was bleeding – the bullet had nicked it.

"Are you still there?" It was Wells again.

"What do you want?" Smith asked him.

"I want you to do exactly as I say. And I suggest you do just that or the next shot won't miss."

"It's over, Wells," Smith tried to slow his breathing. "I know everything."

"I hate talking on the phone. I want you to come up here and we can have a chat face to face."

"I'll take my chances down here," Smith told him. "While I wait for the rest of my team to arrive."

Wells started to laugh. "That's not going to happen, detective."

"They're on their way. It's over."

More laughing.

"The rest of your team is en route to a service station on the A19 via a very clever phone device that my company invented."

"What are you talking about?"

"A message has been sent from your phone alerting them of my presence at a service station. What I need you to do now is get out of the car and place your phone on the roof. And please don't be stupid. You're not stupid are you?"

Smith remained silent. He wasn't sure how much of what Gordon Wells had told him was the truth. How long had he been here? Surely backup ought to have arrived by now.

"Phone on the roof, and then you're going to come up here and we're going to have a chat."

Smith had to think quickly. The rest of his team should have been here by now. He knew that if he made any sudden movements Wells would shoot, but what was waiting for him up in that penthouse? He took a deep breath, opened the door and got out.

"Phone on the roof," Wells reminded him.

Smith did as he was told. He left the phone on the top of his car and started to walk towards the entrance of the apartment block. As he did so, there was a loud crack and his mobile phone exploded on the roof of his car.

CHAPTER FIFTY

"Where the hell is Smith?" DI Smyth said.

Bridge and Yang Chu were crouched behind Yang Chu's Ford Focus. DI Smyth was on his knees behind his own car. They had parked a short distance away from the service station.

"I can't see his car," Yang Chu said.

"How long do we have to wait for armed response?" Bridge asked.

"They're on the way. This man is extremely dangerous, and they are to go in first. We don't want any heroics."

"What exactly did Smith say in his message?" Yang Chu said.

"Just that he'd followed Gordon Wells here and he would wait for us before doing anything."

"That doesn't sound like Smith," Bridge commented.

"The message came from his phone," DI Smyth insisted.

"Something's not right," Yang Chu said. "When has Smith ever waited before tackling a suspect? And where is his car?"

"It must be behind the petrol pumps," DI Smyth suggested.

A white van pulled up alongside them. Four armed officers got out and approached them from the back. One of them – a man with a thick beard looked at DI Smyth.

"What have we got?" he asked.

"Possible sniper," DI Smyth told him. "Almost definitely armed. DS Smith called it in a while ago."

"Is it the deadeye?"

"It could be," Smyth said. "And as such we need to proceed with extreme caution. Smith is in there somewhere."

The bearded man joined his colleagues once more and after a short briefing they set off.

"What do we do now?" Yang Chu asked.

"We wait," DI Smyth told him. "We wait until the area has been cleared and only then do we go in."

"Something's definitely not right," Yang Chu said. "It's too quiet. If Smith's in there somewhere it would definitely not be this quiet. Look. They're coming back."

He pointed to the four armed officers.

"All clear," the bearded man said. "Smith's not here."

* * *

Whitton had managed to contact her dad and he'd offered to pick up Laura from day-care. One of the day-care staff had assured her that Laura had stopped being sick and she seemed to be feeling better. Whitton crossed the bridge over the river and took the side road that led to the new apartment blocks. She spotted Smith's car straight away and realised at once that something was terribly wrong. The front windscreen was gone as was the back one. There was a large dent in the roof. Whitton stopped her car and got out. A few metres away she spotted what was once Smith's phone. It had been blown to smithereens. She crouched behind her own car and took out her phone.

"Where are you?" she asked Bridge.

"Smith sent a message out telling us he'd followed Wells to some service station," he told her. "He's not here."

"He's here at Wells' apartment. His car has been shot at and his phone is in pieces but there's no sign of him."

"Stay where you are," DI Smyth had come on the phone. "We're on our way."

* * *

The doors of the lift opened, and Smith stayed where he was. He leaned forwards and glanced out. The landing was empty. He made his way to

Gordon Wells' penthouse, stopped outside the door and listened. He could hear his heartbeat throbbing inside his head and a dull ache was forming over his left eye. He'd forgotten to bring some tablets with him. He turned the door handle and slowly pushed the door open.

Gordon Wells was standing at the far end of the room. On a tripod in front of him was a heavy-looking rifle.

"It's not quite an L96," he said. "But it gets the job done. Take a seat – I don't need to remind you what I'm capable of."

"You are one sick fuck, Wells," Smith remained standing.

He knew from experience that a sniper rifle was not much use in close combat. He needed to get closer to Wells.

"I told you to take a seat." A bullet flew past Smith's arm and smashed into a table lamp behind him.

Smith moved closer to Wells and as he did so Wells raised his hand in the air. He was holding a handgun and Smith's plan to get closer became useless. He sat down on an expensive-looking leather armchair.

"What are you planning on doing exactly?" he asked. "You realise it's all over, don't you?"

Wells laughed. "It's only just started. Very soon, I'll be far away from here and you'll be dead."

"Why?" Smith decided on another tactic. "Why did you kill all those people? Was it to get back at Robert King or your wife?"

"What do you know about my wife?" Wells now had the handgun pointed at Smith's head.

"I know she was pregnant," Smith replied. "And I know the baby wasn't yours. You can't have kids, can you? That scorpion put paid to that."

"You've been doing your homework. But you don't know anything. Have you ever been betrayed? I mean truly betrayed?"

"I can't say I have."

"Diana betrayed me. She lied to me. She looked at me and lied to my face."
"So, you shot her?" Smith said. "You shot your wife because she betrayed you. And you shot Robert King's ex-wife because she did the same thing to him? Is that right?"
Smith wasn't expecting what happened next. He heard a loud bang and felt a white-hot pain in his arm. He put his hand on the pain and felt the warm sticky blood ooze out.

"Hurts doesn't it?" Wells said.
"I've had worse," Smith tried to remain calm.
The pain in his arm had made him forget about the throbbing in his head. Wells tilted his head as though he was studying an exhibit in a museum. "How did you know? How did you figure it out? Rob was the perfect scapegoat."
"That was your first mistake, Gordon," Smith purposefully used his Christian name. "It was perfect. Too perfect. A killer who murders his victims with such precision wouldn't just leave a sniper rifle lying around for us to find."
"You said my first mistake," Wells said. "Are you implying I made more than one?"
"Killing your wife was your second mistake. You should know we always investigate the husband very closely. Did you really think we wouldn't find out about your past secrets?"
Smith suddenly realised that if he hadn't been so stubborn and insistent, they would not have even looked into Wells' history.

"So, what do you think is going to happen now?" Wells wielded the gun like a conductor in front of an orchestra.
"My guys are going to come rushing in, and you're going to give yourself up. You'll probably spend the rest of your life in prison, but surely that's more preferable to being dead, because that's what's going to happen if you don't give yourself up."

"That's where you're wrong. Don't you think I could have just put a bullet in Rob's head? That would have been much easier, but then he would just be dead. No, this way was much better. I may even have visited him in jail. That would be real poetic justice."

"You wanted him to suffer so much just because he put a scorpion in your bed?" Smith realised that Gordon Wells really was insane. "You killed four innocent people to frame a man for that?"

"Rob King made my life a living hell. Every waking moment was hell when he was around. I hated him before the scorpion, but that was the turning point. Do you have children?"

Smith merely nodded.

"Then you can understand. All I ever wanted was a family. A small piece of me to live on when I'm gone. And King took that away from me. Anyway, enough about me. Do you have anything you want to say? Any last words of wisdom you'd care to impart before you expire."

He started to laugh again.

"Just one question," Smith said. "My wife was supposed to have been with me in the car. What would you have done if she had been?"

"Your wife would be dead now."

Smith looked around the room. The odds were definitely stacked against him. If Wells only had the rifle, Smith may at least have a fighting chance, but the handgun would be a lot harder to beat. On the table next to him was a table lamp and a small vase. There was nothing else within close range that might be used as a weapon. Smith really didn't have a plan.

"I have to be going," Wells told him. "I have a flight to catch. No hard feelings. This is nothing personal."

Smith watched him as he steadied the gun and curled his finger around the trigger. Smith's arm was now numb and the throbbing in his head was taking over again. He looked at the vase on the table – it looked very expensive. He only had one chance to do what he was about to do. He removed his hand from his injured arm and in one swift motion he moved to the side, picked up the vase and hurled it at Gordon Wells. The vase struck Wells on the side of the head, there was a loud bang and a bullet lodged in the wall behind Smith's head. Smith got to his feet and rushed at Wells. He knocked him to the ground and the gun fell out of his hand. The vase was on the floor a few feet away. It was still intact. Wells threw a punch and Smith staggered backwards as Wells' fist slammed into his chin. He felt himself being pushed to the ground and he banged his head hard against the tiled floor. He looked up and saw Wells standing over him with the gun in his hand. Smith closed his eyes.

This is it, he thought. *This is the end.*

    He heard a loud bang and waited for the nothingness to follow.
It didn't happen.
"Are you alright?" It was Whitton.
Gordon Wells was unconscious on the floor next to Smith. The vase Smith had failed to break was now smashed to pieces next to him. Whitton was holding Wells' gun in her hand.
"I think I can feel a migraine coming on," Smith said and got to his feet. "And I've forgotten my bloody tablets again."

CHAPTER FIFTY ONE

Two weeks later

Smith and Whitton were buzzed through the gates at Full Sutton prison and met by one of the wardens. Smith's arm was still in a sling, but he'd been told it wouldn't be for much longer. The events in Gordon Wells' penthouse were still very fresh in his head. He thought he was going to die. Wells had been standing over him ready to shoot. Whitton had ignored a direct order and had gone inside the building without waiting for backup. She'd rushed inside and seen Wells standing over Smith ready to shoot him. She had picked up the vase and hit Gordon Wells on the back of the head with all the strength she had inside her. She'd been issued with a verbal warning for disobeying an order but her husband was alive because of it.

"He hasn't said a word since he was brought in," the warden told them. "If you ask me, he should be in a psychiatric institution, not a prison." Smith and Whitton followed him until he stopped next to one of the cells. "I'll be outside the whole time," the warden said and unlocked the door.

Gordon Wells was sitting on his bunk staring at the wall opposite him. His eyes didn't move.
"Morning, Gordon," Smith said to him. "Do you mind if we come in? We won't be offended if you don't offer us anything to drink."
They went inside. Wells still didn't move.
"This is just a quick visit, Gordon," Smith said. "I wanted to come here in person to bring you a bit of news. I wasn't sure if I should, but I remembered something you said to me back in your flat."
Wells turned to look at him. Then he smiled.
"It's a penthouse." His voice was gravelly.

"Flat," Smith said. "Penthouse. Whatever – it's all one now isn't it? Especially now you're going to spend the rest of your life in here."

"Twenty-five years," Wells corrected him. "I'll probably be out in fifteen. Maybe I'll come and visit you when I'm released."

His eyes moved to Whitton. "But maybe I'll visit you first. How would you like that?"

"I'd love to chat all day," Smith said. "But like I said, I have some news for you. But first, can you remember what you said to me when I asked you what would have happened if my wife had been in the car with me that day?"

"I said your wife would now be dead," Wells said and grinned. "And there's still plenty of time for that. I have years to plan."

"Yes, you do."

"What's this news you have for me?"

"I thought you'd like to know that your wife's body has been released," Smith told him. "So now she can be laid to rest."

"You came here to tell me that? That bitch can rot in hell for all I care."

"They've finished with the autopsies," Smith ignored him. "I just thought you'd want to know."

"Fuck you. I couldn't give a damn about that whore."

"Suit yourself," Smith said. "Let's get out of here, Whitton."

He turned to leave the cell.

Then he turned around. "One more thing, Gordon. I was curious so I asked pathology to check something for me. I did some research and realised that you ought to have got a second opinion after you were told you were sterile."

"What are you talking about?"

"The damage to your private bits wasn't permanent. And the tests I had carried out proved this. The foetus your wife was carrying shared both your